L J WESTON

A PACK OF LIES

SOMETIMES A GRANDMOTHER'S LOVE
IS WORTH MORE THAN A MOTHER'S

L J WESTON

A PACK
OF LIES

SOMETIMES A GRANDMOTHER'S LOVE
IS WORTH MORE THAN A MOTHER'S

MEREO
Cirencester

Mereo Books
1A The Wool Market Dyer Street Cirencester Gloucestershire GL7 2PR
An imprint of Memoirs Publishing www.mereobooks.com

A PACK OF LIES: 978-1-86151-292-5

First published in Great Britain in 2015
by Mereo Books, an imprint of Memoirs Publishing

Copyright ©2016

L. J. Weston has asserted her right under the Copyright Designs and Patents Act 1988 to be identified as the author of this work.

This book is a work of fiction and except in the case of historical fact any resemblance to actual persons living or dead is purely coincidental.

A CIP catalogue record for this book is available from the British Library.

This book is sold subject to the condition that it shall not by way of trade or otherwise be lent, resold, hired out or otherwise circulated without the publisher's prior consent in any form of binding or cover, other than that in which it is published and without a similar condition, including this condition being imposed on the subsequent purchaser.

The address for Memoirs Publishing Group Limited can be found at
www.memoirspublishing.com

The Memoirs Publishing Group Ltd Reg. No. 7834348

The Memoirs Publishing Group supports both The Forest Stewardship Council® (FSC®) and the PEFC® leading international forest-certification organisations. Our books carrying both the FSC label and the PEFC® and are printed on FSC®-certified paper. FSC® is the only forest-certification scheme supported by the leading environmental organisations including Greenpeace. Our paper procurement policy can be found at www.memoirspublishing.com/environment

Typeset in 11/19pt Century Schoolbook
by Wiltshire Associates Publisher Services Ltd. Printed and bound in Great Britain by Printondemand-Worldwide, Peterborough PE2 6XD

CHAPTER 1

Rex banged the front door shut when he left for work, waking me up. It was 6.30 am and I was annoyed because I had a late shift at the supermarket in the evening and needed my sleep. I guessed he was still mad at me from the night before, when I had said I would not tolerate his philandering and wanted a divorce.

I lay there wondering why a man would think it was all right to do what he liked and his wife should not complain. What gave him the right to bed women, from 20-year-olds upwards, and then expect me to welcome him home with open arms afterwards? Was it a middle-aged thing? Rex was 48 years old. Did he think he should sow his oats while there were still some to sow? Did he have something to prove?

Whatever it was, I was having none of it. I wanted him out of the house, and as soon as possible. I would take him to court and get my share of the house and hopefully enough money to get by for a while. I was a forgiving person, but this was something else entirely. Twenty long years wasted on a man who couldn't keep his trousers on!

Besides, at 42 I did not intend spending the rest of my life alone. The very thought of being on my own terrified me. Jane, our daughter, was 15 and was already talking about going to university. I knew that when she did leave the house she might never come back to live permanently with us again. Young adults want to travel after studying for three years, and she was no different from the rest.

That afternoon I had finished tidying up when I heard Jane put the key in the lock and open the door. "Have you had a nice day, dear?" I asked. "How did your geography test go?"

When she didn't answer I went out into the hallway, and then looked up the stairs to see her bedroom door closing. I called out, "Jane, what's the matter? I was asking you how your test went."

I went up, knocked on her door and opened it to see Jane lying face down on the bed sobbing.

"Whatever is the matter, darling?" I asked. "Are you upset over your dad and me? Please don't cry."

She lifted her head and her pretty face was soaked with tears. "Don't cry sweetheart, everything will be all right," I said.

"No it won't, it won't be all right. I'm pregnant." With that she started to howl and scream. I was so shocked. I sat down on her bed trying to take in what she had just said. I didn't even know she had a boyfriend; she had never mentioned that she was seeing anyone.

When her sobbing eased a little, I asked her whether she was absolutely sure.

"Yes - yes, there's no doubt at all. I have done several pregnancy tests and each time over the past few weeks I have tested positive," she screamed again.

Weeks! The word seemed to hang in the air. "Who's the father?" I asked.

"You don't know him," she replied angrily.

"Is he someone in your class?"

"No!" she yelled.

"Where did you meet this person?"

I was determined to get to the bottom of this in spite of her shrieking at the top of her voice.

"At a party a few months ago," she said between sobs.

"Does he go to the same school as you?" I persisted.

"No," she replied with tears running down her face.

"How old is this boy?"

"He's not a boy."

"What do you mean?" I said, fearful of the answer.

"He's a man. He's twenty-five." Jane buried her head once more in her pillow.

"Oh my God. Oh my God!" was all I could say. I was struggling to get my head around it all. But I knew I had to give her all the support I could.

"Darling you are only 15, you are under the age of consent. This man could be in a whole lot of trouble. Have you told him that you are pregnant?" I asked.

"Yes, and I hate him!" she screamed again.

Trying to keep as calm as possible I asked her, "What did he say?"

"He was shocked and said he wanted to marry me next year, but I hate him, I hate him! He has ruined my life. I didn't want to have sex with him, we were just larking about."

"Did he rape you?" I felt I had to ask the question.

"No, not exactly, we had both had a bit too much to drink and he suddenly lost control and it just happened," she said through floods of tears.

"Did he mention that you should have an abortion?" I put the question to her very gently.

Jane screamed at the top of her voice and said "No he wants me to have the baby, but he thought I was older and he's worried because I am under age and he knows he can get into a lot of trouble. He has told me not to tell anyone. He made me swear on the Bible to keep it a secret until he figures out what to do." She turned her face and sobbed into her pillow.

"Well you won't be able to keep this a secret for very long. How far along are you?" I asked.

"Two months," came a muffled reply.

"So that means you won't even be sixteen when you have the baby. Oh my god!"

"Please don't tell Daddy! I won't be able to face him, please Mum," she begged.

"What's the name of this person?" I asked.

"Why, what are you going to do?"

"I'm not going to do anything, but I still would like to know his name and where he lives."

"His name is Patrick, that's all you need to know," she said.

"OK, you just slip into bed and I'll go and make you a nice cup of tea. Things look very black at the moment, but I'm sure we can work through this."

I went downstairs, shaking my head and wondering how on earth we were going to sort this mess out.

I finished my shift at the supermarket and drove home. When I got in I found all the lights on in the house. There were suitcases in the hallway and my husband's overcoat was lying on top of one of them. He came rushing down the stairs.

"Well, you wanted a divorce, and you can have one," he said. "I'm leaving and I'm glad to be rid of you, you nagging old bitch. You'll hear from my solicitor." With that he slammed the front door and was gone. Gone forever, I hoped, never to return.

Only then did it dawn on me how much I would actually miss him, despite everything he had done.

Jane was in her bedroom, collecting her things together on the bed.

"What are you doing?" I asked.

"I'm leaving too, I'm going away," she replied.

"No darling, you can't go away like this, you're not thinking straight."

"I can't stay here, I can't go back to school, what will people say? If I leave now no one will know I'm pregnant. I'll come back afterwards when it is all over, I promise." She flung her arms around me.

"Don't leave like this! Let me ring your Auntie Joyce, go and stay with her, she would love to have you, and meantime we can decide what you want to do about the baby."

"OK you can ring Auntie Joyce, but I've already decided, I'm not keeping the baby. I'm going to have it adopted."

"OK, but I want you to do one thing before I ring Auntie Joyce, and that is, I want you to arrange a meeting for me with this Patrick, I want to speak to him face to face."

"I don't care what he has to say, I'm having the baby adopted!" Jane yelled.

"I'll make this very clear to him when I meet him darling. Is that a deal?"

"OK, I'll stay with Auntie Joyce until the baby is born, but I never want to see Patrick again as long as I live."

Jane left the next day to go to stay with Joyce, my sister in Wales. I saw her off at the station and already I could tell she was looking forward to seeing her aunt. She did not look so worried about the baby, as she had been assured by her Auntie Joyce that she would take care of everything.

I was to meet Patrick when he returned on leave. I had learned that he was a sailor and would not return to Portsmouth for another month, so I had plenty of time to work out what exactly I was going to say to him.

Life was totally different now. With Rex and Jane both gone, my life began to seem empty and meaningless. Maybe I should go back to college and study art; I had always wanted to paint, and in my younger days I had really been quite good at it.

I enrolled at the local college the very next day, before I had a chance to change my mind. I began meeting new people and loving the art lessons, and getting covered in paint was really enjoyable.

Then one evening I looked at the calendar and saw a cross against Saturday 15th. This was the day Patrick would return to Portsmouth. I rang Joyce to ask how Jane was doing and whether she needed anything. I had purposely given her time and space, and this was only the second time I had rung her since she had left.

"She's fine," Joyce said, "I'll go and call her to the phone." I heard her voice in the distance calling Jane. Finally my daughter came to the phone.

"Hello Mum, how are you?" she said.

"I'm fine," I replied, and told her all about the art course I had enrolled in.

"Good for you, you always wanted to be creative, good for you." Jane seemed genuinely pleased that I had taken up a hobby.

"How are you keeping darling, do you need anything?" I enquired.

"Oh I'm quite OK. Auntie Joyce has been really supportive and she fusses around me like a mother hen. I'm really doing well and the doctor says both I and the baby are very healthy," came the very positive reply.

"Well, that's nice to hear. You know, Patrick's due to return on Saturday. I thought I would ring him to set up a meeting, just to let him know that you definitely do not wish to keep the baby and also that you have no intention of ever seeing him again. Unless of course you have changed your mind and want to keep the baby after all, and deal with this matter with him face to face?"

I waited for Jane's reply with bated breath.

"No, I haven't changed my mind Mum. You can tell him that, if you don't mind. I'm thinking of going abroad after the birth and starting a new life far away from here. I plan to go on with my studies and to university later, if I can. Auntie Joyce said she will help me arrange everything after the birth of the baby. Ring me and let me know about your meeting with Patrick, I'd like to know what he has to say for himself. Bye Mum."

That Saturday evening I rang Patrick's number, hoping he was home and settling in after his long stint at sea.

"Can I ask who's calling?" said a female voice at the other end of the line.

"Oh just a friend," I said, " If he's too busy I'll call back another day." I didn't want to sound pushy and I didn't want to attack him straight off. I intended to act calm. I wasn't suspicious on hearing a female voice, as I remembered Jane saying that Patrick lived with his sisters, so I didn't think he had set up house with someone else.

"Patrick, you're wanted on the phone," said the young woman who answered my call.

"Hello, Patrick here, who's calling?" said a hesitant voice.

"Hello Patrick. You don't know me, I'm Jane's mother." I said with a voice full of
trepidation.

I heard a gasp at the other end of the phone. "What do you want?" he said.

"I suggest that we meet. I think we have something to discuss, don't you?"

"Yes, OK. Where do you want to meet me, and when?"

"May I suggest we meet tomorrow in Regents Park, near the children's playground at 2.30? If that's convenient for you." I half expected a refusal.

"OK. How will I know you?" he replied.

"I'll be wearing a light blue suit and carrying a white handbag. Is there anything you can tell me about yourself so that I can recognise you easily?"

"I'm five foot eleven, slim build and have a moustache," he replied in a hesitant whisper. "I'll be carrying a bunch of flowers for Jane."

I arrived at the park early and watched the children playing on the swings. Maybe if things had been different I could soon have been sitting here watching my grandchild playing with the other children, but I knew this would not be the case.

I suddenly became aware of someone standing behind me. "Are you Jane's mother?" said a very polite voice.

"Yes I am, you must be Patrick, how do you do," I said, holding out my hand to shake his.

"Nice to meet you. These are for Jane," he answered, thrusting a beautiful bunch of red roses into my arms.

"Thank you," was all I could manage to say. I thought I would hold back and not tell him immediately that Jane was no longer at home. After seeing him my initial thoughts of an arrogant man taking advantage of a young girl - my daughter - quickly faded. He seemed rather shy and almost childlike.

"How is she?" he asked. "I did write, but she never replied."

I had bundled up his letters and when I thought the time was appropriate I had sent them off to Jane, but she had never spoken about them and neither had I.

"Jane is fairly well, under the circumstances. We have to talk about her and the baby. Shall we walk?"

"Yes, if you want. But I must explain that I didn't know Jane was under age. She looks so grown up in makeup and high heels I thought she was at least eighteen or twenty."

"Well I'm not here to apportion any blame, I just want to try to do what's best for Jane. She wants to have the baby adopted as soon as possible after the birth and she does not want to see you again."

"No, she can't do that! It's my baby and I want my baby. She can't give away my
baby!" Tears welled up in his eyes, and I realised how this whole matter was truly
affecting him.

"That's all very well," I said, "but what means do you have to bring up a baby? Do you own a house, do you have a steady income? And how do you expect to bring up a baby when you're at sea most of the time?"

"I don't know, but I'll try to figure something out. I live with my sisters, but I'll find a place somewhere. I'll be home on leave from the Navy several times before the baby is due, then on a long leave after six months and my sisters will help me raise the baby if I ask them. I want to see Jane, I want to help her. I do love her and I want to make things right if I can."

"Jane has gone away for her confinement and I doubt very much whether she'll be back again, so please don't ring the house for her. I'll tell her what you've said. In the meantime, I'll ring you if the need arises and I'll keep you informed if she changes her mind, which I very much doubt."

I could see the look of despair on Patrick's face. He seemed such a nice guy, someone I would have liked Jane to have as a partner. He had kind blue eyes and a very handsome face.

"If you would let me have Jane's telephone number I could ring her, and maybe persuade her to reconsider," he said. "I know things are a mess, but I'm sure we can work things out."

"I'm sorry, Jane has made it quite clear that she does not wish to see you. I'll tell her what you've said and if there's any change I'll let you know. In the meantime take my work number, and if there's anything more you wish to say I'll pass the message on."

Patrick looked so forlorn. "OK thank you. I'm on leave for three weeks, then I have to return to my ship, but I'll be home again before long, please let Jane know this, and that I'll be there for her if she needs anything, anything at all, please tell her this."

"I will, but I am sure it won't make any difference to her decision about her giving the baby up for adoption."

CHAPTER 2

I continued with my art classes and soon had four paintings ready to show at the local Art Exhibition for Beginners, where there were three prizes to be awarded for the best new artists. At first I thought I wouldn't attend, but then I plucked up enough courage to go along with Mandy, one of the other art students, just to see people's reactions to the diverse collection of modern paintings.

We wandered around like two fugitives, only daring to look furtively at the people who were judging the exhibition. There was one guy who we noticed had spent some time in front of one of my paintings, which was called 'Miriam'. I had wanted to show the young Lady, who had posed for me in a rather seductive way. Although fully clothed, she had ruched up her skirt to her knee and I thought I had captured her mischievous smile.

When the names of the winners were called out later, unfortunately I was not one of them - not that I had imagined for a moment that I would be; I was happy just to have had my work exhibited, the whole scene gave me quite a buzz.

Then something rather unexpected happened. It seemed the man who had been studying my painting had approached the Exhibition Director to ask whether it was for sale and if so, what was the price. The director, who I knew quite well, caught my eye and beckoned me over. He introduced me to the person who was keen to buy the painting.

"Well, er..." I stammered, trying to think of something to say and not having the faintest idea what he was actually asking me. My mind had gone completely blank and I thought for a second that I was actually going to faint.

"Maybe you would like to consider whether you actually want to sell the painting to me? I wouldn't like to rush you into anything," he said. He produced a card from his pocket and handed it to me. "Perhaps you will call me when you have made a decision."

I stared at the card. When I looked up, the man was already moving away and disappearing into the crowd. The director, who had been standing by my side, said, "Well that was a surprise, do you want to sell the painting? And how much do you think you will charge him for it?"

My brain started to return to its rightful place in my head and I replied, "I have no idea, what do you think it's worth?"

"Why not ring him if you want to sell the painting, and ask him to make you an offer?"

That night I turned the card over and over in my hand. 'Philip Rochford, Chief Executive Officer, Preston Oil Company', it read. What a handsome fellow. I thought, I bet he's married with a couple of kids, lives in a fine house in Mayfair and drives a Rolls Royce.

I felt I would happily give him the painting to hang in such fine surroundings, I couldn't wish for anything better. I couldn't wait to speak to him. I decided to ring him the next day and ask him to make me an offer, and then I would say 'Oh that's far too much,' then hopefully he would ask to meet me to negotiate a fair price.

I was so excited at the prospect of talking to Phil (yes, I already secretly thought of him as my friend) that I couldn't sleep. I tossed and turned until daylight.

I waited until after lunchtime before picking up the phone and dialling Mr Philip Rochford's number, but then I quickly put the receiver down. No, this is not the way, I thought. If he comes on the line I'll be stammering and I'll make a fool of myself. Best if I write a few sentences down; that will make me seem more confident, and when he answers the phone I'll be ready to communicate in a really adult way.

"Hello, Mr Rochford's secretary," said a rather pleasant voice at the other end of the line.

"Hello, I'm Mary Wilkinson," I began. "Could I please speak to Mr Rochford? He probably won't know me by name, but I'm the artist he met at the local arts exhibition and he expressed the desire to buy one of my paintings." I was sighing with relief when I had got that out.

"Just one moment please," the receptionist said. There was a short silence and then I heard a familiar voice at the other end of the line. The image I had in my mind was of that tall, dark and very handsome man who was at the exhibition.

"Hello there Mary, nice of you to call. I hope it's all right if I call you Mary?" he said.

"Yes of course, " I replied, without any hesitation.

"Have you decided how much you are going to charge me for that fine painting of yours?"

"Well, I think it would be OK if you just made me an offer," I said rather shyly.

"Sure, that's fine with me. Can you bring the painting to my place this evening and we can thrash out a fair price? Is that all right with you?"

"Yes, that will be fine, " I said, trying not to sound too eager at the prospect of seeing
him once again.

"I'll give you my address, have you got a pen handy? It's 140 Belgrave Square, South West One. Can you make it round about eight o'clock?"

"Yes that will be a good time for me, thank you. I'll see you tonight."

He was probably wanting to make sure the children would be in bed and that he and his
wife would be able to look at the painting in peace before they went out to dinner.

What should I wear? I was very nervous at the thought of visiting Phil at his home. Smart but casual, I thought. I tried on several trouser suits, but in the end I settled for my little black dress, because I felt more comfortable in that. I wrapped the painting up well before calling a taxi for seven o'clock. It was a bit early, but I thought it would be better to arrive early than late. I always hate people turning up late for appointments and I always tried to be on time. I could hang around the corner of the apartment if need be. The painting was not that large or heavy; it was only in a light frame and Phil would surely want to buy a more presentable frame for the painting himself, one to his taste.

At exactly eight o'clock I rang the doorbell of the apartment and Phil's voice came out over the intercom. "Come on up Mary," he said. With that the door clicked open and I made my way to the apartment. I rang the bell, quite expecting a large dog to come bounding out and jumping up on me or to hear a stampede of little feet, but all was peaceful.

"Hello, well done, right on time" said Philip, taking the painting from me. "I like people who are punctual, come on in." No dog, no children and no wife, as far as I could see!

"Let's go into the drawing room, it's brighter in

there," he said. At that moment I would have given the painting to him quite willingly for nothing. It was a beautiful apartment, just as I had envisaged, and I would be happy to have 'Miriam' just hanging on the wall in these beautiful surroundings.

"Beautiful, beautiful, such an attractive subject," he said. "You said I should make you an offer. How about three hundred guineas? Does that sound a reasonable offer to you?"

"Oh yes! that is very generous of you," I replied, not wishing to sound or look too perplexed, as I wasn't sure how much three hundred guineas was, but I think I would have accepted three hundred pennies.

"Let's shake hands then and drink a toast to 'Miriam', he said. "What would you like? I think champagne is in order. Do you like champagne?"

"Yes, that will be fine, thank you."

There was an enormous pop as the cork of the champagne bottle came out, which made me jump.

"And now a toast. To 'Miriam', my first painting of Mary's. May there be more to follow." He looked at me curiously. "Are you hungry? there's a nice little restaurant round the corner. Would you like to have dinner with me?"

Wow! I hadn't expected anything like this to happen. Calm down, calm down, I began to tell myself. This is only an invitation to dinner, he is not asking to marry you. He probably takes people out all the time. I gave quite a measured answer, under the circumstances.

"Oh are you sure? I don't want to keep you from anything."

I can assure you you are not keeping me from anything, Mary."

He proceeded to help me on with my coat and we left the apartment. I could still see no sign that anyone else was living there.

Once inside the restaurant, Phil ordered a bottle of Bollinger. "Is that OK with you? he asked.

"Yes, that's fine." I didn't know one champagne from another, but I wanted to try to
sound knowledgeable and act as if I dined in fancy restaurants all the time.

Phil ordered beef wellington and then a delicious chocolate dessert covered with strawberries and cream with a strawberry sauce. *Please don't let me knock something over or spill the soup in my lap*, I was saying to myself as we sipped asparagus soup.

"More champagne?" he asked.

"No thank you." I didn't want him to think I was a regular drinker. Besides, my head was already spinning.

"What do you do with your time when you are not painting, Mary? he asked. "I see that you're wearing a ring on your finger, so I guess you are happily married?"

"I'm separated," I said instantly, although this was the first time I had ever thought of myself as not being married. I had only slipped off my wedding ring the evening before the art exhibition, and I had soon put it back on, as I had felt naked without it.

Being bolstered up by the champagne I asked him in a confident voice so as to turn the questioning on to him, "And what do you like to do in your spare time?"

"Well, I often lunch with friends. I have quite a few hobbies as well, my main one being golf. And I like going to the theatre," he replied.

Still turning the questioning onto Phil, I said. "I guess you are married? Do you have children?"

"Yes and no," he said. What the hell does that mean, I thought? "Yes I'm married, and no, I do not have any children. My wife refuses to have any children because of her career. She is a doctor and she's dedicated to her profession."

"Isn't that a bit selfish?" I said. "Surely she could have children, then return to work after a few years?"

"You try telling her that. I'm always saying the same thing. Things are not going too well with us at the moment. You see she comes from a very well-to-do family and she's quite spoilt, always thinks she knows best about everything. To tell you the truth I'm getting tired of the bickering and bored with her excuses for not wanting a family. Sometimes I just want to go out to dinner after a hard day's work and relax, just like this evening. Sorry, I didn't mean to go on like that." He sat there reflecting. It was obvious that all was not well with his marriage.

We chatted on for a while and then Phil asked, "Would you like anything else to drink, maybe a liqueur?"

"Oh no, I really couldn't."

"Maybe some coffee then?"

"That will be nice," I said. Although I didn't really want coffee so late, I felt he wanted to stretch the evening out a bit longer. Phil summoned the waiter, who quickly brought two black coffees.

"It's been a real pleasure being with you Mary. I hope we can do this again some time. Maybe we could take in a show in the West End, if you would like to join me?" he asked coyly.

"I would love to," I said with a broad smile, overwhelmed that he wanted to take me to the theatre. Was he asking me for a date? Surely he was!

"My pleasure," he replied.

Outside the restaurant, Phil took my hand in his once again and said that he had had a lovely evening. He then hailed a cab and paid the driver to take me home. I waved goodbye to him as he stood on the pavement and I could still see him standing there fixed to the spot until the taxi turned a corner.

That night I was flying high; not because of the wine, but because Phil was such a handsome kind man, polite and well educated, that I had to pinch myself to make sure I was not dreaming. I felt that he really did like me very much.

Next morning I was awakened by the flap of the front door and the sound of something heavy being dropped on the mat. Rousing myself from the very little sleep I had managed to get, I went downstairs to find a large white envelope lying by the front door. It looked very official, and sure enough it was. It was a solicitor's letter telling me that my husband was filing for a divorce, and there was a whole wad of divorce papers with it.

My first feeling was of great sadness and loss, but after several coffees, with a slug of brandy in each, I began to feel that a heavy burden had been lifted from my shoulders, and I gradually started to feel quite happy. Maybe it was the brandy.

I flicked through the pages and found that the gist of the paperwork was that my husband wanted a quickie divorce, and he was offering to pay towards Jane's upkeep until she came of age. I could keep the house until Jane was 18; it should then be sold and the proceeds split equally between him and myself. There was no mention of any other money.

Great, I thought. I had a few thousand stashed away, and a good clean break was the ideal way to part. Now I could get on with my life.

Jane kept in touch as she had promised. There were no problems so far with her confinement. She had had a scan, and discovered that she was expecting a boy. She sounded almost pleased when I spoke to her.

"Does this mean you've changed your mind about keeping the baby?" I asked her.

"Certainly not!" came the terse reply.

"I see," I said, trying to calm the situation. "Not long to go now darling. Should I come along to be with you at the time of the birth?"

"No, Auntie Joyce says she will be with me at the hospital during the delivery and I'll leave as soon as possible afterwards. I have already seen someone about the adoption."

"I understand. Your father has filed for a divorce. He's agreed to let us keep the house until you are 18."

"Well, I've made up my mind. I'm going abroad to study, maybe to Canada, so I'll not be living in the house. And Mum, I want you to promise me that you won't tell anyone after I have gone - about the baby I mean. I want to make a fresh start, and some day I hope to get married. I'm not going to let this baby spoil my life. On the birth certificate I'll just put 'Father Unknown'".

"What about Patrick?"

"Well what about him? He can hardly object now, can he?"

I felt I should not antagonise her and I said, "I suppose not. Can you put Auntie Joyce on the line darling?"

"Hello Mary, how are you?" came Joyce's normal happy tone.

"Hello Joyce, I'm just fine. I wanted to ask you to do me a favour and let me know as soon as Jane gets near her time and before she goes into labour, that you will ring me. I want to be there. Look, I want you to keep this a secret. I'm concerned about the baby and I want to see that he goes to a good home. He is my grandson after all."

"OK Mary," Joyce whispered. "I'll phone you when the time comes."

CHAPTER 3

A few weeks later I picked up the phone to hear Patrick's voice.

"Hello Mary. What's the news about the baby - you must have heard from Jane. Can we meet?" He sounded nervous, but excited.

I said I was happy to meet him, but I didn't really think there was anything I could do to ease his torment over the baby. Patrick came to the house, and I made dinner for him. I didn't broach the subject at all, and neither did he, until after the dessert.

"Does she still want to have the baby adopted?" he asked.

"Yes. She still feels this will be best for her and the baby. She's having a little boy."

At first Patrick's face beamed with pride that he was about to have a son, but then reality set in and his face fell. "I see," he said. I sensed that he was resigned to what was going to happen to his little boy.

I felt that I had to tell him that Jane was determined to enter on the birth certificate 'Father Unknown', and Patrick readily accepted this, I guess because Jane was so young, although Patrick wanted to make one last effort to try to have some connection with the baby.

"What can I do?" he pleaded. "I'll do anything. I want my baby."

I knew Jane would not change her mind on this. I began to feel deeply sad about the whole affair, for Patrick and about not being able to see my grandson grow up.

"Tell me what to do!" he begged. He put his head in his hands and sobbed out loud.

"There is still a while to go," I told him. "Leave things with me. I can't promise anything, but I'll do my utmost for you. I know you genuinely want your son. Maybe there is a way. I'll try to see the Adoption Agency right after the birth."

Why was I trying to give him false hope when I knew very well that he didn't stand a chance of getting the baby?

After that Patrick and I started seeing one another regularly when he was on leave to discuss the baby. He started to bring me flowers when he came to visit and we spent many hours not just talking about the baby but about other things, about the exotic ports where his ship docked, about the beautiful beaches where the sailors would swim when they were off duty. I was quite fascinated and spellbound at the stories he had to tell, and as time went by I felt a growing attachment to Patrick. Was I falling in love with him, I asked myself?

We both felt very relaxed in each other's company, and one day when we were out walking he suddenly turned to me and said, "Mary, why don't you adopt the baby? It is only a suggestion. I'll pay for his upkeep and I'll make regular visits to help out. We seem to get on well and I know you don't want to lose your grandson."

At first I thought it was a preposterous idea, but then the more I thought about what Patrick had said, the more I came round to the idea that I really could look after the baby myself, with his financial help.

I saw Patrick several more times before the birth of the baby and suddenly I found myself planning a future with the baby and a real growing attachment to him. I was considerably older than he was, 17 years to be exact, and yet when I was with him that age gap really didn't seem important. I would soon be divorced, and I started believing that I really could raise my grandson and bring him up as my own. Patrick was such a dear, and I felt he would make a wonderful father and a wonderful partner.

Was I being silly, daydreaming that we could live as a couple? What was I thinking of? Patrick had only offered to financially support the child; he hadn't asked to marry me. Men often marry or live with much younger women, but not the other way around. I pondered over the question of whether I could raise a child again at my age and what to do about Phil. I still liked him very much, but I had not seen or heard from him in quite a while.

I knew he had marital problems, as on our last meeting together he had told me that he didn't want to stay with his wife, but at the same time she had told him that she would not give him a divorce. Things sounded very messy between them. I was very reluctant to phone
him, as I didn't want to come between him and his

wife, and I certainly did not want to be cited in any divorce proceedings should things go to court. I had to think carefully now about the baby.

The very next day Patrick phoned to say he wanted to meet me that afternoon, because he had something he wanted to ask me. What could this be I wondered? Perhaps he wanted me to try for the last time to change Jane's mind about giving up the baby as the due date was nearing.

Before Patrick could say anything, I told him that I had applied to the Adoption Agency to adopt the baby as a blood relative. As there was no father, at least no known father, according to the files, I had asked to be his adoptive mother. I was told I would have to wait until the necessary forms had been completed and filed, and although the Adoption Agency thought this highly unusual, they did not see any problems.

He immediately said he wanted to be the adoptive father.

"Let's get married and make it all legal," he said. "I'm very fond of you and I think we would make a very happy family."

Although I had thought of Patrick as a partner, it still came as quite a surprise when he actually proposed. I looked into his eyes, which were full of anxiety and steeped with sadness. I could tell that he was going through hell. I decided to accept his proposal. Although he didn't say he loved me, it was very early days. Being fond of me would do for now.

Patrick phoned me every day throughout the whole of the next week, asking me whether I had contacted the Adoption Agency to let them know that I was getting married. I purposely delayed telling them, as I had to be sure I was doing the right thing and to give Patrick time just in case he changed his mind.

When I contacted the Adoption Agency and told them of the news, they said that we should both attend a meeting soon after the wedding.

Joyce rang me to say that Jane had gone into labour, and I immediately left for Heathrow Airport and Wales to be with Jane for the birth. Jane's son arrived safely, and as soon as the hospital gave permission for her to leave she moved to a friend's house 50 miles away.

She didn't see or hold the baby after the birth

and was behaving as if, as far as she was concerned, he didn't exist. I told her before she left that I was thinking of adopting him to bring him up at home, and if I was to keep her secret about her pregnancy she would have to keep my secret, about her not living at home. If her father knew she was not living in the house he would expect me to sell it and divide the proceeds as soon as possible. She agreed.

My divorce had become final, and after a very short courtship, Patrick and I were married in a local Registrar's Office. I didn't tell Jane; I decided to wait for some time in the future when she was more settled. She had enough to deal with, and besides she might have gone crazy at the thought of her mother marrying the person she hated so much.

We attended the meeting with the Adoption Agency and were told that everything had been finalized to give me and Patrick the son we both dearly loved to us, to raise as our own. After a few formalities of form filling the baby was placed in my arms, and Patrick and I gazed down at our beloved son. He had a shock of blond hair and the most beautiful blue eyes you have ever seen.

We decided to call the baby Christopher. It was

Jane's grandfather's name, my ex-husband's father. I felt it was appropriate because it would keep the ties to Jane, the baby and to her grandfather, who she adored.

Patrick had to spend a few more months in the Navy, but I didn't mind as getting to know Christopher (Patrick called him Chrissy for short), and becoming a mother again after such a long time was a joy. It was not easy, especially getting up in the middle of the night for feeds and changing, but I soon got into a routine.

I kept my job working in the evenings, employing a local girl to be with Christopher during the time I was working. She was a single mum and she brought her one-year-old daughter with her and was very glad of the extra money.

One night there was a call from Phil.

"Hi there, I was wondering if you would like to come with me to the theatre," he said. "It has been a while since we met and I have some good news to tell you."

My first thought was to say "No it's too late. I can't, I'm married," but I was a bit lonely with Patrick away and after all he was only a friend.

We met the following Saturday evening and went out to dinner first. After we had sat down, he took my hand in his and told me that he had filed for a divorce.

"But your wife had refused to divorce you," I said immediately.

"Well she changed her mind after realizing it was futile trying to hold on to something that no longer existed between us."

I was wondering what he was going to say next. I was so dumbfounded at this revelation that my mind was not able to process all the thoughts that jumped into my head.

"Well, don't you have anything to say?" he asked, smiling.

"Oh yes, I answered. "Congratulations must be in order. You weren't happy and I think you've done the right thing. You were living separate lives. No use staying married just because you once loved each other. Things change, people change and life is too short to stay in a disastrous relationship."

All the while I was thinking to myself that surely he couldn't be thinking of walking back into my life after such a long absence.

"I wanted to get in touch with you sooner Mary, but my work had taken me abroad on urgent business," he said in a rather apologetic way. "Do you have any news about your divorce?"

"Yes. We decided to split amicably, and it's all over and done with now."

I wasn't ready to tell him about Patrick and Christopher - besides, it wasn't any of his business. I hadn't seen him for months. How dare he think he can walk back into my life after such a long absence! I would just look upon him as a friend, I thought.

We saw a wonderful play and it was a very pleasant evening.

"How's your artwork coming along Mary? Any new paintings you want me to take a look at?" he asked over coffee.

"No. I don't think I have any which would be suitable for you, just old buildings and café scenes. I'll let you know when we have a new exhibition and you can view all the new paintings."

When Phil brought me back home, he didn't seem to want to leave me. Previously he had shaken my hand and said goodnight, but this time he stepped out of the taxi with me and escorted me to my door.

"It's not easy to get a taxi from around here," I quickly blurted out. "Best not let the taxi go. We can meet some other time, I'll ring you."

He obviously got the message. He smiled and took my hand in his and gently planted a kiss on the back of my hand.

"I've had a wonderful time Mary, please don't leave it too long before you get in touch," he said. "Good night."

"Good night, and thank you for a lovely evening," I muttered.

I paid the babysitter off and flopped down on the settee. If only he had got in touch with me sooner, things could have been a lot different, I mused. Well it was too late now, far too late. I couldn't change things now.

A couple of months went by and I didn't phone Phil. I thought it best to distance myself from him. Things could not go anywhere and life was complicated as it was. Patrick would finally be demobbed in two weeks' time and I had every intention of making a go of my life with him and Christopher.

The phone rang early one morning and hesitantly I picked up the receiver. There was a familiar voice at the other end - my daughter's.

"Hi Mum, it's me. I hope you haven't forgotten that it's my birthday today."

"Of course not, "I quickly said. "Happy birthday darling. What are your plans for today? Will you be coming home for a visit soon?"

"Well my friend and I are going to Paris for the weekend with her parents and then hopefully, I'm going to Canada in the autumn. I need you to sign the forms which I've sent to you. I can't study in Canada without at least one parent's consent. I hope to study at a good college in Toronto and then go on to uni to do an art course."

"OK darling, I'll get the forms back to you as soon as possible. In the meantime, have a wonderful birthday and a great holiday. I miss you very much. I hope I'll see you one day when you're ready to pay me a visit."

I held the phone, hoping to continue the conversation, but I heard a click at the other end of the line. After a few seconds I replaced the receiver. I stared at the carpet for a while. It was beginning to dawn on me for the first time that I was losing my daughter. Maybe I would never see her again. No, I couldn't let this happen. I would sign the forms when I got them and go to see her before she left for Canada. I couldn't let her go like this.

I kept my eye on the calendar and gave Jane a week to collect herself after her holiday. A neighbour had generously offered to look after Christopher for the weekend, so after phoning Joyce, getting Jane's address and swearing her to secrecy, I boarded a train for Pontypridd in Wales.

I knocked on the door of the little cottage and Jane stood aghast in front of me.

"Well, a hug would be nice," I said. "I've come all this way to bring your forms to send off to Canada."

"Oh you shouldn't have come, you could have posted them to me," she said. She then gave me an enormous bear hug. "It's really lovely to see you Mum, you're looking really well. Come in, the place is quite small, but cosy. Patsy is out shopping, that's my friend, and this is her pad. Her dad pays the rent so I'm really fortunate in that respect."

She fussed about making tea for me and was rather chatty, almost her old self, but she didn't ask after Christopher. She still acted as though he didn't exist, and I thought maybe for her at least it was better that way.

I left around five o'clock after meeting Patsy, who seemed a very nice girl and was going with Jane to Canada to study. I knew it would be a long time before I would see Jane again, and when it was time for me to leave I burst into tears.

"Don't cry Mum, time will soon pass and I'll be back," she said. She had called a taxi for me and I cried all the way to the railway station.

I was still sobbing inwardly when I reached home. I cradled little Christopher in my arms and was so glad that I had this little bundle of joy.

The phone rang and it was Patrick.

"Hello Mary. Just ringing to let you know we'll be docking tomorrow," he said in a very excited tone of voice. "Can't wait to see you and little Chrissy. How are you both?"

"We are both well and looking forward to having you home for good," I replied and I put the receiver to Christopher's ear. "Say hello to daddy," I said. Christopher squealed and blew a few bubbles.

"Did you hear your son?" I said to Patrick.

"Yes I did, I am thrilled to hear his little voice, I can't wait to get home to you both."

Patrick was so pleased to see Christopher that he scooped him up in his arms and whirled him around, giving him an 'aeroplane ride', which Christopher loved. He squealed with excitement. He then gave me an enormous hug and kiss. It was very plain to see that he had genuinely missed both of us.

With tears of joy in his eyes Patrick said, "I couldn't wait for the time to pass to be home with both of you, I've really missed you two, but that's all done with now. Now we can be together all the time and be a real family."

"You'll miss the sea, and going to all those exotic ports," I said.

"Well that phase of my life is over now. I'm looking forward to a new beginning. I'll take two weeks' holiday and then I'll look for a job."

"What job are you going to apply for?" I had no idea what skills Patrick had, and I realized that even now I knew very little about him.

"I like carpentry. Maybe I'll find myself a job in a furniture factory," he replied.

I wasn't very impressed with that choice of work, but I wasn't going to worry about that just now. I was so pleased to have Patrick home with me and Christopher.

Patrick, Christopher and I lived a happy and peaceful existence for a while, with Christopher going to half-day nursery and Patrick happily doing what he liked in the carpentry business, while I was back working on my next art exhibition. I had some very fine paintings, I thought, to display, and couldn't wait for the showing, which was only a few months away and was already being advertised.

One Friday evening when I was upstairs getting ready to go to work, the telephone rang. Patrick answered it.

"Who was that on the phone?" I asked.

"I don't know," he called back. "It was a man's voice. He wouldn't give his name or say what he wanted, he just put the receiver down. I guess it was a wrong number." I wondered whether it was Phil.

Six months after that I received a letter from Jane saying things hadn't gone too well at the college and she had got herself a modelling job. She said she and Patsy had gone their separate ways, but that she had made new friends in the fashion business and was earning a lot of money. I was a bit concerned about her, being so young, but I guessed there was little I could do about it as I knew she would not want to come home.

Then my ex-husband rang unexpectedly one evening when Patrick and I were just about to watch a video. "Hello, can I speak to Jane?" he said.

At first I was taken aback. I hadn't expected Rex to phone asking to speak to Jane, although it was only natural he would want to speak to his daughter one day, but Jane was about 4,000 miles away, and come to think of it, why had he not in fact phoned before to find out how his only child was doing?

"Can you hold on a second?" I said, and clasped my hand over the receiver while I thought up something to say to him. I asked Patrick not to make a sound.

"Hello, are you there Mary?" Rex went on. "I want to speak to Jane, can you put her on the phone?"

"I'm afraid she's gone out, Rex." I decided to pluck up the courage to call him by name, although the word was like poison in my mouth.

"Oh that's a pity. She was supposed to keep in touch with me and I haven't heard anything from her in a very long time. Please ask her to ring me, I have some good news for her."

"I will," I said and put the receiver down. I must have gone very pale. Patrick looked at me and said, "What's up? Looks like you've seen a ghost."

"That was Rex asking to speak to Jane. Things could get a little awkward with her being in Canada, he thinks she's living here. If he finds out she's living abroad he'll ask me to sell the house and give him his half of the proceeds."

"Really, I didn't know that you still had ties with your ex," Patrick said.

"Yes, I'm afraid so, only over the house until Jane is 18," I quickly added. "I'll settle with him then once and for all. I'll have to phone Jane. Perhaps somehow she can ring her father without revealing where she is, but it's going to be very difficult."

I rang Jane straight away, as I knew I wouldn't be able to sleep with this hanging over my head. I was lucky she was getting ready to go to work. It was only early afternoon in Canada and she was not on call until the evening show.

I told her her father was asking after her and that he had asked for her to phone him as he had some good news to tell her.

"Well you know what that is," she said. "I guess he's had a brat and wants me to congratulate him."

"Oh, I never thought of that, do you really think that's why he phoned?

"Yes of course, why else?"

"Suddenly I felt very jealous. "How are you going to contact him without him knowing you're out of the country?" I said, rather uneasy.

"Well that shouldn't be too difficult, I have a friend who works at the telephone exchange. He'll patch me through somehow," Jane replied confidently.

"Is everything OK, with the modelling I mean?" I was trying not to sound worried.

"Yes it's great, I'm loving every minute of it."

"Please remember our promises to each other Jane," I said, trying not to sound too worried. "I don't want to give up this house, at least not for a while yet."

"I won't say a word about anything Mum, trust me, Dad won't know that I'm not in the country."

"OK darling, keep in touch."

"Bye Mum, I'll ring you soon," she said and replaced the receiver.

It was a lovely day and I decided to take Christopher to Green Park instead of our usual place. I thought I would walk through to Buckingham Palace to show Christopher the guards, and if we were lucky perhaps they would be going through their paces in the Changing of the Guards, quite a spectacular event. We were lucky enough to catch the end of the ceremony and Christopher was absolutely delighted.

He was now at an age when he was getting more observant. He loved the soldiers and squealed with delight, along with all the other children looking through the railings of the palace.

After a while I headed towards St. James' Park to show him the ducks on the pond and the pelicans, thinking I would perhaps grab a coffee from one of the stalls. I was fishing through my purse to find some change for the coffee when I heard a familiar voice.

"Hello Mary, fancy seeing you here." I turned

around to see Rex standing by my side with a pram. Sure enough, Jane had been right. He did have a new baby, a girl. She was wearing a bright pink bonnet over a mass of curly blonde hair.

"This is my daughter Fiona, " he said.

"Congratulations, "I stuttered.

"And who is this little lad?" He was smiling at Christopher in his pushchair.

I wanted to blurt out, 'This is your grandson, you've always wanted a son, well now you

have a grandson who you will never know, thanks to your infidelity,' but fortunately I

came to my senses.

"Oh, this is a neighbour's child. Just doing her a favour taking him out while she is at the hairdresser's. Well, I must be off, she will be wondering where I've got to with her baby. Nice to see you are keeping well." Although I hated the sight of him I thought I would try to be civil on the surface. "Bye," I said with a wry smile.

"Bye" he replied.

I abandoned the coffee and quickly made off with Christopher. I didn't want to hang around in case he started asking me who the neighbour was - he knew most of them.

He called after me, "I spoke to Jane, thanks for that."

CHAPTER 4

My paintings for the exhibition were the best I had ever done. I had spent many hours at the art college perfecting my work. Patrick had not minded me being away from the house, as he had joined a darts club and was entering a tournament, which I was glad about. Christopher was being looked after by his usual carer, who he now called Nana. I had three paintings to show and I was very excited trying to imagine what reaction I would get and also if anyone would want to buy them.

I also wondered whether Phil would be there; I hadn't seen or heard from him for a long time now and I still valued his friendship.

The day of the exhibition arrived and I tried on one dress after another.

"What are you doing?" Patrick said. "You're not

going to a cocktail party. Look at the bed! You must have tried on about six dresses."

"Oh, I'm so nervous." I replied. "I want everything to be just right."

I put on a blue dress, which was the first one I had tried on. "Are you coming tonight, Patrick?" I thought I would invite him, although I already knew what his reply would be.

"Sweetie, I hope you don't mind if I give it a miss. You know it's not my thing and besides there's an amateur darts match I've entered and I rather fancy my chances with these local guys," he said. He had turned his back to me so that I couldn't see his face, but I thought he was lying. The room had filled with his aftershave, which was never a good sign.

"OK," I said, "I hope you do well."

I arrived at the exhibition centre five minutes before time to find that there were a good few people there already. I spoke to some of my art colleagues and they all seemed to be as nervous as I was. I spotted Mandy, who was nervous, but excited, and said she had seen my work displayed at the back of the hall, which I felt was rather unfortunate, as sometimes people only stayed around the entrance and the first line of paintings where there was free wine to be had.

I walked around to the paintings at the back of the hall and it was a few seconds before I spotted my paintings, almost hidden away in one corner. Not many people would notice them there, I thought.

Just then I heard a voice behind me say, "You look as if you need one of these."

I whirled round to see that it was Philip (although I called him Phil in my private thoughts, I did not feel the time was right to be too chummy). He was holding out a glass of red wine, which I took without hesitation. My heart was leaping about and doing somersaults.

"Beautiful work, absolutely fantastic!" he said. "I have already been round the hall as I was the first one here, and there's nothing to compare with your pictures. Now are you going to sell them to me? I want all three paintings, name your price."

My hand was shaking and the wine was getting sloshed about in the glass. I took one big gulp before Philip took it and put both glasses down on a bench. He grabbed me by the hand and led me to the main entrance.

"My car is just around the corner," he said. He dropped my hand and put his arm out for me to take, which I did without hesitating. I turned round to see Mandy holding up a 'SOLD' sign with an enquiring expression on her face. I nodded to her and with my free hand I raised three fingers. I knew she would dash round to the back of the hall and put the 'SOLD' stickers on all three paintings.

The restaurant was quite busy, but Philip was well known there and the waiter found us a nice private corner. Philip said he had made several trips to the Middle East, where the company had acquired two new oilfields which seemed to be showing signs of large quantities of oil after only a few test drillings. He was heading back to the Middle East in a day or two, as soon as he had sorted things out in London.

"How long will you be gone?" I asked him, not wanting to sound too anxious.

"Just a couple of weeks, if all goes well. In any event not more than a month, as I have meetings back here then."

After we had eaten, he took my hand in his and said how much he had missed me. I looked down and realised that I had my wedding ring on my finger. It was the one Patrick had given to me, but fortunately it was almost identical to the one I'd had from Rex. I had been wearing that one when I had first met Philip, and I only hoped he thought it was the same ring.

"Well Mary, how much do you want for the paintings?" he asked. "I'm looking forward to hanging them in my apartment along with the first one."

"Philip, I told you, you can have them as a gift. I do not want any payment. I would love you to have them and to know that you will appreciate them."

"Well, we will talk about that later," he said.

Philip called me a taxi and kissed me goodnight, saying he would be in touch as soon as he was back in the UK. He asked me to have the paintings delivered to his apartment.

Mandy was on the phone first thing in the morning enquiring about Philip and how the evening had gone, as I had confided in her that I was very fond of him, but we could only ever be just friends. After she had heard all the details about our evening, she couldn't wait to tell me that another couple were very interested in my paintings. I was thrilled, as I hadn't been sure whether Phil was wanting the paintings because he really liked them, or whether it was because he liked me.

A few days later Patrick picked up the mail and handed me a letter.

"Who's that one from?" he asked. I opened the envelope to find a brief note inside saying, 'I hope this amount is OK for the paintings'. With it there was a folded cheque for £3,000.

Patrick was hovering around me asking over and over again what the letter was about, but I managed to put the note and cheque back into the envelope without him seeing it.

"Oh, it's just a note to say that someone was interested in my paintings and wanted to know how much I wanted for them," I said, turning my back to him just in case he saw my flushed face.

This was my first lie to Patrick, and I felt a little guilty, but I had my suspicions about what he was getting up to at the darts club, as on a few occasions he had not come home until 2.30 am and I knew the matches were over well before midnight.

Christopher was growing up fast, and the cheque from Phil would be extremely useful for his clothes.

I kept most of the money hidden from Patrick and didn't spend anything on myself, as I couldn't face answering lots of questions from him about expensive clothes and where the money for them had come from.

I kept my eye on the calendar, wishing the next few weeks would fly by until I could see Phil again. One evening I was standing in front of the calendar when Patrick came into the kitchen. In fact his aftershave entered ahead of him; he seemed to have had a bath in it.

"I'm off to the darts club, don't wait up," he said.

"So you expect to be quite late then?" I said.

"Yes, you know what it's like when the lads get together and have a few beers, time flies by."

He had not kissed me goodbye for quite a while now, and this time he left the house without a backward glance. I suppose I had been expecting too much in thinking our relationship would last a long time. I had made every effort and we had been happy for a while, but I guess Patrick was looking for someone much younger now and felt assured that I wouldn't be going anywhere. After all, I was heading for my fifties, and who wants to be bothered with a fifty-year-old woman with a baby?

I felt the only thing keeping us together was Christopher. Patrick did love him very much, I knew this from the start of our relationship, but I had hoped he would eventually come to love me as well. I guess it wasn't to be, and it had always been a marriage of convenience for him.

I was sure Patrick was having an affair - or was I imagining all this? I had no proof. After all, some men do like to splash aftershave on themselves, even if they are not up to anything. But the situation was highly suspicious and I wanted to get to the bottom of it, even if I didn't like the outcome.

I showered and changed. I was determined to find out what Patrick was getting up to, and if he was having an affair, I needed proof now, not six months down the line.

I hit on a plan. I asked my neighbour to babysit for me after 9 pm. She thought it was a funny time for me to be going out, but I said something urgent had come up. I got to the club around 9.30 pm and sat in a dimly-lit part of the room. It was crowded, and I noticed Patrick straight off. He was throwing his darts at the board, and then someone declared him out. He then sat down in one of the front row seats with his mates cheering the next player on. I needn't have worried, I thought, he was innocently playing a game of darts as he had said, and I became rather cross with myself for not trusting him. What a silly person I had been.

I watched him for a while and I was about to leave when I saw him get up and go to one of the booths. There were two girls sitting there, a redhead and a blonde. The blonde girl smiled at Patrick and got up and left. Patrick sat down and put his arm around the redhead and beckoned the waiter over. He ordered some drinks, then nestled up to the redhead and started kissing her ear and neck. This went on for some time. When they had finished their drinks they got up and left by a side door.

I sat for a few moments, feeling very jealous and full of rage. Then I got up and left the club and walked about for a while, telling myself that for the second time I was facing the end of a marriage.

My thoughts turned to Christopher. He was only just two, and I made up my mind that I would fight tooth and nail to keep him. He was my adopted son, and I was not going to lose him. My mind was a jumble of thoughts. What a swine! Why had I been caught out a second time with such a philandering sonofabitch?

That night I tossed and turned in bed, checking the clock every few minutes. It wasn't until 4 am that I finally heard the key in the lock and saw a light under the bedroom door. Should I confront him now, or should I leave it until the morning? Why should he flop into bed and have a good night's sleep while I lay awake all night? He was the one who was in the wrong, I told myself. As soon as he opens the bedroom door I'll put the light on and confront him.

I waited and waited, but he didn't come to bed. I threw the covers off, put on my dressing gown and went downstairs. Patrick had gone to sleep on the settee, and he was out cold and snoring quite loudly. As I stood looking over him, I was full of rage. I wanted to jump on him and beat the living daylights out of him.

The tears started to well up in my eyes and then run down my cheeks, I felt so absolutely miserable. I wiped my nose and decided to confront him in the morning when I would be calm. If I woke him up now he would be in no fit state to know what time of day or night it was.

I passed a restless night and got up feeling exhausted. Finally I hauled myself out of bed and went downstairs to find Patrick eating breakfast.

"Why did you sleep on the settee last night?" I asked him.

"Oh, one of the lads was hurt in a car crash and I spent most of last night at the hospital, he was badly shaken up, I didn't want to wake you."

I thought I would play along to see where his lies would take him.

"Is he all right, is he badly hurt?" I said, not believing a word he was saying. I kept thinking over and over in my mind, 'What kind of fool do you think I am?'

"Yes he's fine. He got off with just a broken leg, he was lucky." He kept his head bowed, not looking up once from his breakfast, not daring to look me in the eyes.

"Was it Richard? I have heard you mention him in the past," I said.

"No, it's not one of my darts mates. It's Adam. I've spoken to you about him, if you remember." His face began to flush a little.

"Which hospital is he in? I said quizzically. "I think we should go and visit him today just to make sure he's all right. You don't mind if I come along, do you?"

"No that will be OK, but I think we should leave it a while as a lot of his mates will want to visit him in hospital. There's plenty of time, we can go later on, perhaps see him when he comes out of the hospital." Patrick lifted his head and gave a wry smile.

Over the next few weeks I was trying to decide what to do about Patrick, who had said nothing more about going to see Adam or whether he had been to see him by himself. I was one hundred per cent sure that he had made the whole thing up to cover up his late-night dalliances with the redhead, but I thought I would bide my time before confronting him.

One evening when I was feeling very low, knowing full well that Patrick was out seeing his redhead, Phil phoned.

"Hello, how's my girl?" he asked. It was the first time he had addressed me in this way.

"All the better for hearing your voice," I answered, and I meant it.

"Things are going to take a bit longer out here than I expected," he said. "At the moment I'm out in the field, but I just had to ring you, I wanted to hear your sweet voice. I've missed it so much."

"What's that noise? Are you playing football?"

He laughed heartily. "I knew you would cheer me up, darling" he said. "No, I'm out in the oil field in Kurdistan, sweetheart, it's not a football pitch, that's the wind you can hear. There's a bit of a storm brewing." I had forgotten for a moment that he was an oil man. "The government here are delaying us over drilling rights, licences and the like, but we hope to sort this mess out very soon and then I'll be home."

"Oh I'm sorry, you must think me an awfully stupid person," I said.

"No, I think you are intelligent and very gifted," he replied. "I don't expect you to know anything about this place. All you need to know is that it's usually very dry and dusty and extremely hot during the day, but the nights can be very cold. Mary darling, I just wanted you to know that I love you and I'll be with you soon." He spoke in a very romantic tone of voice. "I had just stepped outside to tell you this so none of the other chaps could hear me, but I will have to go as the dust storm is getting worse and I need to get inside. Bye darling, I will ring you again soon."

With that the phone went dead, But I was feeling ecstatic. Phil had said he loved me and missed me. Wow! That was all that I could think of to say to myself.

Then realization dawned on me. What about Patrick? What was I going to do about him, and what was I going to tell Phil about him?

The very next night I was awakened by a noise downstairs in the kitchen - it was the washing machine. Why on earth had Patrick put on the washing machine? I looked at the clock; it was 4.30 am. I went downstairs to find him tossing in his sleep on the settee.

On entering the kitchen I saw a belt on the floor, and beside it were some spots of blood. Had Patrick hurt himself? And why had he put the washing machine on in the middle of the night? I stood transfixed. What had he been up to? Had he been in a fight?

I could see Patrick's shirt, jeans and jacket being

sloshed around in the machine. My first instinct was to clean the floor. I picked up the mop, but then I stopped myself just in time. I didn't want to be an accessory to anything Patrick might have done. I had to think of Christopher. Who knows what he has been up to?

I closed the kitchen door quietly and went upstairs and drifted off back to sleep.

I was woken at 6 am by a hammering and shouting at the front door. "Police, open up!" came a loud voice. I ran to get Christopher, who was screaming. I picked him up and stood at the top of the stairs with him in my arms.

Patrick opened the door and several police officers spilled into the house. "Are you Patrick Stevenson?" one of them asked him. Patrick took a few steps backwards, looking startled but also, I thought, guilty.

"Yes, I am. How can I help you, officer?"

"We are arresting you in connection with the murders of Mr and Mrs Stoppard, You don't have to say anything..." The officer went on reading Patrick his rights.

My head was spinning. What had he done? The policemen were now moving all over the house, into the kitchen, two into the dining room, and one was coming up the stairs towards me.

"Are you Mrs Stevenson?"

"Yes," I replied, "and this is my son."

"We are taking your husband in for questioning in relation to two murders which took place in the early hours of this morning. My squad will need to take some samples of blood found in the kitchen for forensic examination. It won't take long, but we need your full co-operation, please madam." He spoke in a very stern voice.

Stunned, I just nodded my approval. Patrick looked back and yelled over his shoulder to me, as the police were escorting him out of the door. "I'm innocent, Mary. I'm innocent!"

I watched speechless as they bundled him into one of the waiting cars.

By seven the police had left and the house was quiet again. I sat down, still shaking, with Christopher in my arms and sobbed into his little body. I tried to pull myself together, as he was beginning to cry along with me.

I noticed that the police had left a card on the coffee table. It had the details of the local station and a phone number which they had invited me to ring.

I went into the kitchen to give Christopher his breakfast and saw that the washing machine had been emptied. The belt which had been on the floor the previous night had gone, but there were still a few spots of blood on the floor.

When I took Christopher to the bathroom, I found that the cabinet had been ransacked. Medicines were in disarray, with antiseptic bottles on the edge of the sink and others strewn her and there. Spots of blood were smeared on the cabinet door.

Once I had settled Christopher down for a nap, I picked up the card and telephoned the number.

"Hello, this is Mrs Stevenson," I began. "Can I please speak to the Inspector? My husband is helping with enquiries into the deaths of Mr and Mrs Stoppard and it is important that I speak to the Inspector handling this case."

A man's voice came on the line. "This is Chief Inspector Morgan. What can I do for you, Mrs Stevenson?"

"I would like to come along to the station to see

my husband, I'm sure there must be some mistake," I said. "My husband is not a violent man and I wish to be by his side during this stressful time."

"I'm afraid you will not be able to see your husband for a while, Mrs Stevenson, he is undergoing questioning and is not allowed visitors. We'll let you know when you can visit him."

As soon as the Inspector stopped talking the telephone was promptly disconnected.

I was desperate to talk to someone, so I telephoned my sister Joyce. When I told her what had happened and about my suspicions about Patrick's affair, she went very quiet.

"Are you there Joyce?" I said.

"Yes, I'm listening Mary. I'm so shocked I'm lost for words. How long has this affair been going on between Patrick and this woman?"

"I suspect for a while now," I said, "at least a few months that I know about."

"Oh Mary, that's terrible!" she replied. "Do think carefully before you do anything, you have Christopher to think about."

"I know. I was waiting for the right time to have it out with him. Well, it looks as if that time has now arrived. As soon as I can see him I'll let him have his say and then I'll tell him that I have known about the affair for some time and I've seen him with the redhead with my own eyes. He's been so cunning, hiding this from me. I'll tell him that I want a divorce and that I'll be keeping Christopher. I won't stop him from seeing Christopher, as he does love him so and he is his father after all, but it will be on my terms and when it's convenient for me."

When I had finished talking to Joyce I telephoned the police station again and was told that Patrick was being held for 72 hours, after which time he would either be released or charged with murder.

Three days later Patrick arrived home, looking pale and drawn.

"They've released me, but they've asked me not to leave the area as I may be called in for further questioning," he said.

"Well, perhaps you'll tell me exactly what's going on. I tried to come and see you on the first day of your arrest, but they said you weren't allowed any visitors."

He seemed full of remorse and held his head in

his hands. "I've been such a fool. I never meant to hurt you, it was just a bit of fun at first and then Ruth, the woman I met at the club, began to get serious about our relationship."

"Start at the beginning Patrick, I said, "I want to know everything."

"OK, I'll tell you." He sat down and started to talk. He confessed to seeing the redhead, who he had met at the club. Her name was Ruth Stoppard.

"One night she asked if I would drop her home and then she invited me in for a nightcap," he went on. "She said her husband was away and he wouldn't mind anyway as he had girlfriends. We were just friends for a while, then she became very amorous one summer's night and seduced me in her garden between the hedgerows. It happened out of the blue. I did try not to see her, but she was rather persistent. I kept telling her I was happily married and wouldn't leave my wife and son." Patrick started to pace up and down in the room. "Then the other night her husband came home and caught us together in the kitchen. He went berserk. He started grabbing knives from a kitchen block and throwing them at both of us, one after another. He hit Ruth with one of them, but I managed to duck out of the way. It was like you see those men in the circus throwing knives at a woman being spun on a wheel, he was like a man possessed. He caught me on the arm with one and blood started to spurt down my shirt and trousers. One knife hit the tiles and landed beside me, and when I saw him lunging at me with a carving knife in his hand, I picked the knife up from the floor and defended myself. That's all I did, I was just defending myself. It was him or me, he was like a mad dog.

"I stuck the knife into him, I knew I only had the one chance. I asked him to back off, but he kept saying he was going to kill me. When he fell to the floor I ran for the front door and once I was out of the house I phoned for an ambulance."

Tears were now welling up in Patrick's eyes, and he was breathing heavily.

"I stripped off when I got home and put my bloodstained clothes in the washing machine and disinfected my arm in the bathroom. I wrapped a bandage tightly round it. You know the rest. I was sent to the hospital to have my arm stitched under police escort. The forensic test on the blood in our kitchen proved it was mine and no one else's. I'm sorry Mary, I know you must hate me, I don't deserve your love, please try to forgive me."

Patrick was now sobbing loudly and holding his arm, which I knew must be giving him a lot of pain. He went into the kitchen to get a glass of water and took two tablets which the hospital had given him for the pain.

"How long have you been seeing this Ruth woman?" I asked.

"Only a few weeks, I swear."

"Stop lying to me Patrick. You see, I came to the club one night and saw you with her. It was at least two months ago. I watched you for some time kissing her and embracing her and I saw you leave the club together." I spouted the words out at him like a venomous snake.

Patrick's face went bright red and he stammered out, "Well it may be a bit longer than what I said, I don't remember the exact date I met her."

"Patrick, you have lied to me and cheated on me. I want you to pack your things and leave this house immediately. You have deceived me for the last time. I'll be filing for a divorce. I'll let you have access to Christopher, but it will be on my terms and when it's convenient for me." I felt like hitting him. Had it not been for his injury I probably would have done.

He put his head in his hands and began to sob like a baby. "Please don't send me away Mary, I love you!" he cried.

"Well I must say you have a very strange way of showing it. I have made up my mind, Patrick. We're through. I can't possibly live with you after this. I'll tell the police we've decided to separate and it's up to you where you go. You'll have to let them know your new address."

Patrick picked up the phone and called one of his sisters to ask if he could stay with her, then he phoned the police to say what had happened and told them he would be moving to a new address. I think the police were considerate and realised Patrick's predicament; they asked him to phone them back the next day and to check in daily to the police station. It didn't look as though he was completely out of the woods yet.

He then left, taking some of his belongings with him, and said he would collect the rest later.

CHAPTER 5

I called in at the decorators to redecorate our bedroom, as I felt I could no longer sleep there as it was. As a matter of fact I didn't want to live in the house at all any more, so I decided to put the property on the market. At least I would not have to lie any more, and if I gave Rex his half of the proceeds, that would cut the tie with him. I could perhaps start a new life with Christopher somewhere else, far away from the memories of this place and my two cheating husbands.

Then, out of the blue, Jane rang and dropped a bombshell on me.

"I'm getting married," she announced with great excitement.

"Oh Jane, you are too young! Can't you wait a bit until you have travelled and done the things you always said you wanted to do? Have you given this enough thought?" I said. "I don't want you to make the same mistakes that I have made."

"Yes Mum, I have given the matter a lot of thought and Don is the right person for me. I'm absolutely sure about this. Mum, you may not believe me when I say that he is such a loving and caring person. He is wealthy and handsome. He is a fashion designer and a bit older than me, ten years to be exact, but I don't see that as a problem. He's very kind and he simply adores me." Jane was gushing with praise for her future husband and sounded very excited. "You will come to my wedding, won't you Mum? It's going to be held in New York."

" Oh Jane, I don't know what to say."

"Oh and Mum, I forgot to tell you, Don is an American citizen and we'll be living in America, California probably, but we'll be travelling a lot to Paris and Milan, because his work takes him all over the world. I would love you to be at my wedding Mum, it will be in four weeks' time. please come! I'll send you all the details in the post. I love you lots, have to go now, see you soon, bye."

She hung up before I had a chance to ask her

whether she had been in touch with her father and whether she had invited him to the wedding. Maybe a trip abroad was just what I needed. I thought it would get me away from all this trauma. I could leave the sale of the house to the estate agent, and Rex could help with it. After all, he should work for his money and he would surely get the best price for the house.

I decided to start packing and boxing up my belongings. Not only would it keep me busy, it would take my mind off things.

Suddenly I felt alive with renewed energy. I telephoned Joyce to give her the news and asked her to look after Christopher for me while I was away.

"No way, I'm coming with you," she said, in a determined tone of voice. "I wouldn't miss Jane's wedding for the world. We can take Christopher with us, it won't be a problem."

"Oh, I'm not so sure about that," I said. "You know how Jane has always felt about Christopher, and I wouldn't want to upset her on her wedding day." The mere thought of a family row at such a time filled me with horror.

"They must have babysitters in America, for

goodness sake! It will only be for one day. Jane will never need to know he's there, and besides, I know you, you would be worrying about him all the time if you left him here. You just leave the arrangements to me. I'll phone Jane and let her know we are both coming. Just make sure Christopher has had his jabs and that you're both fit to travel." Joyce was always so strong and confident and so dependable.

"Joyce, you are a wonderful sister and friend," I said. "I know I can always rely on you."

"I'll be only too pleased to help out and I'll enjoy it so much. I'm already getting excited at seeing Jane. So must you be, It's been a long time since you last saw her. I bet she's grown into a beautiful woman. I'm not sure about the age gap between her and her future husband though." Her voice was now full of scepticism.

Patrick phoned to ask whether he could collect the rest of his things from the house, and I told him that he would have to come straight away as I was leaving for the USA for a holiday; I thought it best not to say too much to him. I had already packed up the rest of his belongings and they were lying in the hallway for him to collect. He tried to engage me in a conversation about how bad he felt about what he had done, and would I reconsider taking him back once I returned from holiday. I told him I would think about it, but I really had no intention of going back to him, I just wanted him out of the house.

The time went by very quickly and I was checking my list of things to do before leaving the house for the airport. First I had to inform the estate agent that I would be away for two weeks. I left them Rex's number to contact in an emergency. I presumed he would be around. Then I had to check passports, money and visas. I hoped I was doing the right thing taking Christopher with me.

Finally I had to phone Phil. I picked up the phone and dialled his number, but there was no answer.

The taxi arrived and we were at last on our way. Joyce would be meeting us at Heathrow Airport and had phoned me to say that she had left Cardiff Airport earlier in the morning.

When we got to the airport, she came running towards us, dragging her suitcase. She seemed ecstatic.

"Hello, my darlings, how are you?" she said. She hugged Christopher and me, and couldn't believe what a beautiful little boy he had become. Although I had regularly sent photos of him to her, I guess in the last six months I had been a bit lax and not really kept this up.

Finally we were in the air and on our way to the USA. It was a long flight, but thank goodness Christopher slept most of the way. Joyce had booked us into a nice hotel off Broadway. I phoned Jane to say that we had arrived safely and Joyce got in touch straight away with an agency to arrange for a nanny/babysitter for Christopher. We interviewed three young ladies and we both agreed on a 22-year-old called Donna who was training to be a nanny.

The next morning we left Christopher with Donna while we went out shopping; she planned to spend the day getting to know him and taking him to Central Park. We each bought an outfit for the wedding and Joyce bought a lovely blue suit for Christopher. Joyce insisted on buying the suit for him as she had not sent him anything for his second birthday. I said it really wasn't necessary as I had brought along several changes of clothes for him and he would only be romping about in the park. I only hoped it would fit him when there was a suitable occasion for him to wear it.

When the day of the wedding arrived, Joyce and I were up very early getting ready and telephoning Jane to see how she was coping. We had as yet not seen her, but she had asked us over for a pre-wedding breakfast. She wanted Joyce and me to get her ready for her big day.

We made sure Christopher was settled with his babysitter and had plenty of toys to play with, then we left for Jane's hotel near Park Avenue. She had a lovely suite at the hotel and there were beautiful young ladies coming and going, some with their hair just done, while others were on their way down to the hotel salon to have their hair done and a makeover.

The reunion with Jane was overwhelming. "Now don't cry Mum or you'll make me cry too, and I don't want to be a red-eyed bride," she said. "Have some breakfast, it's all laid out in the other room. Then you and Auntie Joyce can go down to the salon for your makeovers. There's no rush, we don't have to leave here until 11.30 so there's plenty of time."

"Did Jane say we are booked in for a makeover?" Joyce asked between bites of her scrambled eggs and miniature sausages. "I've never had a makeover before."

"Neither have I," I said, "I'm so excited."

The six beautiful girls were Jane's modelling friends, and all of them were getting ready to be Jane's bridesmaids. There was one little boy who I had thought to be the son of one of the bridesmaids, but when I asked about him I was told that he was Don's son and he was being dressed as a pageboy.

"Did you hear what that young lady said, Joyce?" I told her. "The little boy is Don's son."

Joyce's mouth fell open. Thank goodness she had finished her breakfast.

"He's been married before and has a son?" she enquired, with a look of disbelief on her face.

"Yes, so it seems."

One of the bridesmaids, Juliet, accompanied Joyce and me down to the salon and while we were waiting our turn for the makeover she revealed that Don had in fact been married before and that his wife had died in a car crash about a year and a half ago.

"That's not very long ago," I said to her.

"Jane and Don knew each other for some time before his wife's accident, they worked together. Jane has been modelling Don's gowns for quite a while. Don thought it best not to wait too long to get married again on account of Simon, he needed a mother."

I looked at Joyce and immediately I could read her thoughts and she could read mine. We were both flabbergasted. How was it possible that Jane could not be a mother to her own son, although she had been very young at the time, yet take on the role of mother to someone else's? She had always seemed not to show any parental love in the past.

It seemed I didn't really know my own daughter after all. I was quite overcome with emotion and felt quite bitter towards Jane. I also felt very, very sad for Christopher.

I later learned that Don had been driving the car which had caused the death of his wife, and that left me feeling rather sick in my stomach. Were they arguing at the time, I wondered? Was he having an affair with Jane at the time? Could the same sort of thing happen again?

I asked Jane whether she had invited her father

to the wedding. "Yes" she replied. "But he said eighteen was too young to be getting married and he couldn't understand why I was getting married in New York. However, he sent his blessings and said he was unable to attend because of another engagement."

Joyce telephoned the babysitter to check on Christopher before we left for the church. The wedding was to begin at 12 o'clock and at 11.55 all the cars carrying the bride and ensemble arrived at the church. Jane looked so beautiful. I only wished her father could have been there. Two rather handsome men were standing at the altar, and with Jane on the arm of another dashing man she led her bridesmaids down the aisle.

Joyce and I took our seats in the beautiful church and then the wedding ceremony commenced. After all the introductions and congratulations, we stood for the photographer on the steps of the church. I was only hoping that I would be able to conceal my rage for Jane on this, her special day.

"Has Jane asked about Christopher?" Joyce asked.

"No, not a word. I think she's removed any trace of him from her mind," I replied.

"I don't know how she has managed to do that, especially knowing that Christopher and Simon are more or less the same age."

Jane and Don left for their honeymoon early in the evening, together with Simon, who Jane held in her arms like a doting mother. They were off to Milan for two weeks before flying to Paris for the new season's fashion show.

Joyce and I had time to see some of the sights of New York in the days after the wedding, but I was glad when it was time to board the plane for home.

"Do you want to see the wedding photographs?" Joyce asked, after we had settled ourselves in our seats. She handed me a brown envelope. I flicked through them and handed them back to her.

"Not so fast, you surely couldn't have looked at them properly," she said.

"Yes, I've seen them."

"Look again, over to the right of Jane," Joyce insisted. I didn't know what she was getting at; there were people there with children who I didn't know.

"Don't you recognise anyone?" Joyce was pointing her finger at a woman with a child in her arms. "You didn't know that Christopher attended his birth mother's wedding, did you?"

I looked closer, and sure enough it was Donna, the babysitter, with Christopher in his new blue suit.

"Did you arrange for them to be there, Joyce?" I asked.

"Yes, I did. I gave the babysitter the time and venue of the wedding and asked her to squeeze into one of the shots. Isn't it nice to see three generations of the family together?"

Jane of course would have been oblivious of this. In her wildest dreams she would not have known that the child she had given birth to was at her wedding.

Christopher fell asleep after his dinner on the plane and Joyce and I tried to get as comfortable as possible for the long night flight home.

"Where are you going to live once you have sold the house?" Joyce asked me. "Have you got somewhere in mind?"

"I thought I would like to live in a small cottage in Surrey, if I can find one which is suitable for Christopher and me, but of course it will have to be near a school and not too far from a railway station. I don't want to break my links with London entirely," I mused.

"That sounds like a good plan, considering you have all your friends in London."

Unknown to me, Phil had returned to London in my absence and had phoned me to ask me out to dinner. He was surprised that after several attempts over several days he was unable to contact me. He later told me that he had driven to my house to find a 'For Sale' board in the front garden. He had rung the doorbell and Rex had answered. Rex had said, "Hello, have you come to see the house? The estate agent didn't tell me you were coming."

"No," Phil had said, "actually I was trying to find Mary, I'm a friend of hers. I've just arrived from abroad and I wanted to speak to her." Not being sure of the situation, he hastily added, "I bought some paintings which Mary had exhibited at the local hall and I wanted to speak to her about them."

Rex had invited him in, and told him that I was

in New York at the present time at our daughter's wedding. "She should be coming back soon," he informed Phil.

Phil did not stay long as he felt awkward talking to Rex, although he found him to be hospitable enough. He left after a few minutes, leaving Rex a card for me to give him a call when it was convenient.

Joyce and I were both feeling rather jet-lagged when we arrived back at Heathrow Airport. Joyce had just enough time to collect her luggage and then race round the airport to get her connecting flight to Cardiff, but before she did so, I asked her to watch Christopher while I made a quick phone call to the house to see if Rex was there. I didn't want to arrive home with Christopher to face more questions. It turned out that he was there, but said he was only picking up some of his things before leaving once and for all, as he had managed to find a buyer and everything was going through nicely.

"The sale should be completed within a month," he said. "Where are you going to live, Mary?"

"I haven't found a place yet, but I'll be moving

out of London and probably going south of the river. I'll give the estate agent my new address," I replied.

"Will you be living alone?"

What an impertinent question, I thought and hastily added, "No, I have a person in my life named Christopher and we're going to make a new life together." I added under my
breath, *not that it is any of your business.*

"Good, I'm glad to hear that, if you need to contact me you have my number. The solicitor will deal with the money side of things and the proceeds of the sale will be split fifty-fifty. Good luck."

Not having heard from me for a while, Phil had returned once more to the house just as Rex was throwing a bag in the back of his car. When Phil pulled up he noticed that the 'For Sale' sign had been changed to 'SOLD'.

"Congratulations," he had said.

"Oh, yeah, things are moving quickly now," Rex had replied.

"I wasn't able to reach Mary and I have to leave today for the Middle East," Phil informed Rex. "Perhaps you'll see that she gets my new telephone number."

Phil handed Rex his new card. Although Phil wanted to put the card through the letterbox, he felt a little awkward with Rex standing there.

"OK, I'll do that," Rex had replied.

"Will she be moving close by?" Phil had asked.

"No, she says she's going south of the river and she's setting up home with the new man in her life. His name is Christopher."

Rex got into his car and waved Phil goodbye. Then he threw Phil's new card with his new phone number on it into the glove compartment and drove off.

Phil had stood on the pavement feeling quite stunned at the thought that I had a new man in my life. All his hopes of sharing a life with me had been dashed. He got into his car without a backward glance and drove off, feeling a desperate sadness at the prospect of never seeing me again.

It must have been only a few minutes after that that my taxi drew up outside the house. I found Phil's card on the table and excitedly dialled his number, but there was no reply. I tried many more times over the next few hours, but the line seemed to be dead. I felt too exhausted to try any more that day and began to settle Christopher down in what would now be temporary accommodation.

It wasn't long before I found an ideal cottage down in Surrey, just the kind of place I had always dreamed of living in, literally with roses round the front door. I enrolled Christopher in a local nursery and took a job in a dental practice, working as a receptionist from 9 am to 3.30 pm. Christopher loved his new nursery and new friends. Although the children were made to sleep for an hour at the nursery in the afternoon after lunch, Christopher was always ready for his bed after his six o'clock bath and was tucked up in bed by 6.45 pm.

I couldn't get Phil out of my head and almost every evening when things were quiet in the cottage I dialled his number, but it was always dead. I turned the card over in my hand, wondering why he had left this number for me to ring him, when it wasn't connected to the exchange. I rummaged through my handbags and found a previous number for him, but that number didn't ring and there was no engaged signal either; it must be another disconnected line.

One afternoon when I had finished work a little

earlier than usual, I plucked up enough courage to telephone his office.

"Hello, Preston Oil Company," came a charming voice from the other end of the line.

"Could I speak to Mr Philip Rochford? I'm a close friend of his," I said.

"I'm afraid Mr. Rochford is out of the country" came the reply. "He won't be back for some considerable time."

"When exactly will he be back?" I asked.

"I believe he will be away for two years." Shocked and almost crying I said, "That's an awfully long time, are you sure?"

"Well I shouldn't really be telling you this, but he felt there was nothing to keep him here after his divorce, so he took on the supervision of a new oil find out in the Middle East."

"Thank you," I said. I put the phone down, trembling. The words 'Nothing to keep him here' rang in my ears. Was I really nothing? I had thought we were good friends, more than friends. I had thought he had true feelings for me, had I misread the situation? Was he just interested in my paintings after all?

I picked up the calendar and scribbled 'TWO YEARS' across the whole of the month of May.

It was some time before I managed to settle down to a life with Christopher. I had always thought there would be a chance of a loving man coming into my life. I must admit that I began to feel a little bitter towards men in general, and if anyone made advances towards me I would quash them instantly. Men soon learned to stop talking to me if they tried to chat to me when I was out with friends for the evening.

One morning a package arrived, and I put it on the coffee table to open later in the day. I had to drop Christopher off at nursery school and then get to work, and I didn't want to be late.

That evening I opened the brown envelope to find the official divorce papers, which Patrick had already signed, ending our marriage. I guess my silence over his hope of some reconciliation had convinced him that it was all over between us. Another failed marriage, I thought. There was also a letter from him in which he said that he was full of remorse at the ending of our marriage and wanted me to forgive him for the affair with Ruth Stoppard.

He asked whether he could come to see little Chrissy, as it had been some time since he had seen him. 'Please let me know when it will be convenient,' he wrote. He went on to say that he had been cleared of all the charges in relation to the deaths of the Stoppards.

I didn't want Patrick around me or Christopher, but on the other hand I didn't want this visit hanging over me. If I refused to let him come, he might well start custody proceedings, and I couldn't bear the thought of losing Christopher. So the sooner he came to see Christopher, the better.

I signed the papers that evening and wrote Patrick a short note saying we could meet up at the weekend at Richmond Park. There was no need to reply; I would be by the main gates at 2 pm on Sunday. I had to find out whether he was going to file for custody of Christopher. I telephoned Joyce and told her about my intended meeting with Patrick.

"You've done the right thing" she said. "Just get it over with, then he can't complain that you've stopped him from seeing Christopher."

A few days later I had a letter from Jane saying that things were not going too well with her and Don since they had returned to New York. She seemed to be constantly left with young Simon, while Don was out most evenings. It wasn't what she had planned at all. It wasn't clear whether things would improve, but at the moment she was clearly rather unhappy with married life.

I did not write back to Jane, as I was still annoyed with her for taking on someone else's child while she had never accepted her own, but I was surprised that things had already begun to go wrong with her marriage.

That Sunday Christopher and I waited by the main gates of Richmond Park for Patrick. Christopher was very excited at the thought of seeing his father, who was a few minutes late and blamed it on the trains. He picked Christopher up and spun him around, kissing him on both cheeks. He had brought him a ball to play with and they were soon happily kicking it about in the field.

After a while we sat down and Patrick told me of his plans to emigrate to Australia.

"I have been cleared of all the charges against me" he said. "So I'm now free to travel. My sisters and I want to start a new life down under, but I will keep in touch with you on a regular basis to see how Chrissy is getting on, if that is all right with you."

"Yes, of course," I replied. "I do hope everything works out for you all."

"So do I. I hope you'll send me photographs of Chrissy and keep me up to date with his progress in school, when he starts there. I'll make sure to send him birthday presents and Christmas presents. Perhaps one day he will be able to visit me," he added hesitantly.

Thank god he never mentioned fighting for the custody of Christopher. I could now breathe a little easier.

"When will you be leaving?" I asked.

"Not for a couple of months yet. It will take that long to settle everything up."

I was happy to hear the news, purely for selfish reasons, but I wished him well and said that he could visit Christopher any time he came to England. I asked him whether he would like to attend Christopher's christening before he left.

Although this had only just popped into my head, I thought it would be nice for Christopher, Patrick and his aunts to be together before they left for Australia.

"When is the christening?" he asked.

"I'm waiting for a date from the church, but it shouldn't be long now. Can we agree on a full name for Christopher? I thought that as Christopher is Jane's grandfather's name perhaps we could have his middle name as Scott, which is your father's name. Christopher Scott Stevenson - do you think that sounds OK?" I asked.

"More than OK, it sounds just right. Christopher Scott Stevenson - yes, I like that name very much, sounds very distinguished. Let me know as soon as you have the date and time and I'll inform Martha, Betty and Susan, they will all want to be there."

"And I would love Christopher's aunts to be there too," I replied.

Patrick kissed Christopher and kissed me on the cheek, saying "See you soon then." Then he waved us goodbye.

On the way home I called in at our local church. Evening service was in progress and I waited until everyone had gone before speaking to the vicar. I told him that Christopher's father was going abroad and I wanted to have Christopher christened as soon as possible.

"Well I do have a slot" he said, "but it won't be until the middle of next month, the 16th to be exact after morning service at 11.45 am. Shall I enter that in the register for you?"

"Yes please." I replied.

I phoned Patrick as soon as I got home and he promised to be at the church on that day. I informed Joyce that Patrick was planning to go to Australia and told her the date of the christening, and she said she wanted to be there.

"What should I buy for Christopher to wear for the christening?" I asked. Normally children who were christened were young, babes in arms, and they would wear a little white or cream gown. Christopher, being two and a half years old, would be a bit of a handful, and probably wouldn't stand still for five minutes. Joyce suggested the little blue suit that we had picked out for him in America would be just fine, and it would bring his birth mother into the frame as he appeared in her wedding photographs wearing the suit.

"That's it then, that's sorted," I said.

The day of the christening soon arrived and I introduced Joyce to Patrick. "How do you do? I have heard a lot about you," said Joyce.

"I'm sorry it hasn't been all good, but I aim to change," replied Patrick.

Joyce just smiled, and I introduced her to Patrick's sisters. She thought Christopher was the image of Susan, the youngest sister, who was blonde and blue eyed, just like Christopher.

The christening went smoothly and Joyce and Martha, the eldest of Patrick's sisters, became godparents to Christopher. It was lovely and sunny when we arrived back at my cottage, so we were able to have brunch in the small garden area. Christopher was busy opening the presents he had received from his aunts, Patrick and me. It was a lovely occasion and I felt that Christopher at last had a family he could be proud of. We took lots of photographs and I promised I would send Patrick copies as soon as he forwarded me his address in Australia.

CHAPTER 6

As the months went by I decided I needed some sort of outlet, as I was not meeting people and was feeling very low. I decided to occupy my time by joining a large studio where several painters worked. At first I would stare at the empty canvas and my thoughts would always be with Phil. I tried to blot him out of my mind and decided to paint scenery instead of portraits. I sloshed the paint on the canvas and was quite engrossed in what I was doing, until I felt a tap on my shoulder.

"May I ask what this is?" asked a man's voice. It was the Art Director of the studio, and he was looking at me quizzically.

"This is a landscape," I answered.

"OK - you have green paint for the grass?" he queried.

"Yes, that's right," I replied.

"Is that a little brown hut?"

I nodded.

"And I take it this is the sky?" I nodded again.

"This is very unusual, I have never seen a sky look like this" he said. I had subconsciously splurged black paint over most of the canvas, broken up by streaks of bright red. "This looks very unnatural indeed. What's the matter Mary, are you in some dark place and taking it out on the canvas?"

On reflection my picture did look like something a psychopath might have painted, and I began to realise how bleak it looked. I threw down the brush and ran out of there and headed home, feeling sure that my days as an artist were well and truly over. I paid the babysitter for looking after Christopher, then I crashed out on the settee and wept.

The trouble was, I couldn't get Phil out of my mind. I missed Patrick and I even missed Rex; all the men in my life had disappeared. My life was in turmoil and for days I had been like an automaton, dropping off Christopher at nursery, making appointments at the dental practice and going home to an empty cottage. I was going through a very bad patch in my life and didn't know how to get out of it. The only thing I was sure about, the only thing that kept me sane, was my son.

The next evening the phone rang. "Hi there, this is Mandy, I hope you remember me. It's been a long time since we spoke, how are you?" she said.

I had just put Christopher to bed and was about to spend another evening sobbing on the settee.

"Mandy, how nice of you to call. Oh, I'm fine." I was only hoping I didn't sound too depressed.

"How's the painting going? I'd love to see your latest masterpiece."

"Oh no you wouldn't" I replied. "Even my Art Director got a fright when he saw it."

Mandy laughed loudly over the phone. She just thought I was joking.

"Guess what, I ran into an old friend of yours in St. James's Park today. He was just sitting there reading a newspaper, I wasn't sure at first if it was really him, but as I got closer I was sure. Hard to forget such a handsome man. Any guesses?" she said in an excited tone.

I just listened, not daring to hope.

"Well, I won't keep you in suspense any longer, it was Philip."

I couldn't breathe. I was so overcome with emotion that I almost put the phone down.

"Mary, are you there?" she said. "Make some noises so that I know I'm not talking to myself".

"Yes, I'm here," I said.

"Well, I said to him, 'Aren't you Philip? I'm Mandy, you don't know me but you bought some paintings at a gallery near here, quite a while ago now, and the artist is my friend Mary, and I remember seeing you there." And he said, 'Oh, how do you do, and how is Mary?" I of course said that I hadn't seen you in a long while, but that you were now living in Surrey. He asked me if you had married the new man in your life, Christopher, and I burst out laughing and said 'Christopher is a little boy who Mary adopted'.

"Well you should have seen his face! He went white, he went purple and then he went red. Are you there Mary?"

"Yes. Wherever did he hear about Christopher?" I said.

"Apparently you said that you had a new man in your life to Rex, and he told Philip."

"No, no, I didn't say that."

"Well he had given his new telephone number to Rex when he saw him leaving the house, and Rex promised to give it to you. Philip had to leave his apartment in Belgravia quite suddenly, as his wife became unbearable just before his divorce. He then rented an apartment for a while, and he left that telephone number on his first visit to your house, then he left his new number for his new apartment in Westminster with Rex. You didn't get in touch with him, and he didn't know where you were, so he took a job working abroad for two years."

"Oh my god! It's all been a horrible mistake!" I said, bursting into tears.

"Well, I think Philip knows that now, and I have given him your new address and phone number so I'm sure he will call you. He said he was only back for two weeks."

"Thank you so much, Mandy, I'm so grateful to you."

"It's a pleasure, my darling, I hope you guys get together soon."

What a shock! I sobbed and sobbed. I couldn't believe that it had all been through a terrible mistake that Phil had taken a contract abroad. I was so exhausted and relieved about the whole episode, and quite euphoric. I sat staring at the carpet for a while with Mandy's words still ringing in my ears, and then I gave in to my tiredness and fell asleep on the settee.

After a while I realised I had heard a knock on the door, but I felt far too groggy to answer it. I looked at my watch and realised that I had slept for quite some time. I could not rouse myself enough to answer the door.

"Go away!" I yelled out, but then the bell rang. I thought that if I didn't answer the door, Christopher might wake up. I dabbed my eyes and shook myself awake and went to open the door.

I was almost bowled over to see Phil standing there with a bouquet of red roses in his hands. For a few seconds I couldn't move or say anything. He must have come straight down to Surrey from London after speaking to Mandy.

"These are for you," he said. "May I come in?"

I burst out crying at the sight of Phil. I took the

bouquet and asked him to come inside. After I had placed the bouquet down on the coffee table, Phil spun me around and held me in a tight embrace, kissing me longingly and lovingly.

"I have missed you so much, my darling," he whispered in my ear. "So very much."

We stood for a few seconds in each other's arms, just hugging each other, not wanting to let go. Then I realised what an awful fright I must look with my puffy, dark-ringed eyes. I settled Phil in the lounge while I went to the kitchen to put the flowers in water and also to splash some water on my now very swollen eyes.

When I rejoined Phil I told him everything that had happened in the past, not leaving anything out. I told him all about the lies that had been told, some to protect other people. I also told him about all the cheating that had gone on, not keeping anything back. I wanted to purge myself of the false life I had been living for so many years. I knew I was taking a chance that he might walk away, but it was a chance I had to take.

Phil seemed quite stunned at what had been going on in my life and did not seem to be able to comprehend that people could live their lives in this way. I didn't feel worthy of him, and quite expected him to get up from the settee and walk out of the door; he would have been quite justified in doing so. Instead he took my hands in his and said, "Mary, don't reproach yourself. You have tried to protect your daughter and most of all your grandson at the risk of your own happiness and you should be commended for your actions." He planted a kiss on my forehead as a father would a child.

"Oh Philip, I have missed you so terribly, and I've yearned for this day for so long. My brain has been in torment. I didn't know what to think when I found out you had gone abroad for two years."

We chatted until the early hours of the morning, and I took Phil to see Christopher in his bedroom. "He is such a bonny little lad, I can't wait for him to wake up," he said with such eagerness.

Phil spent the night with me, and for the very first time I realised that I was truly in love. I pledged to him that I would never lie to him, even to keep someone else's secret, and he promised that our future would be a loving, caring and completely honest partnership.

After breakfast Phil got down on one knee and asked me to marry him, saying he wouldn't take no for an answer. I said yes immediately, and told him it would be an honour to be Mrs Philip Rochford. From now on I would call him Phil, and confessed that unknown to him that is what I had always called him.

After playing with Christopher for a while, Phil gave me the keys to a new apartment he had bought in Westminster for us, which he had purchased when he had left his marital home in Belgravia and had been living in rented accommodation, before he thought things had all gone wrong between us and he had left to go abroad to try to forget me.

He reaffirmed what Mandy had said, that he had to leave again for the Middle East, but would spend the rest of his leave with me and that he would not leave my side until the day of his flight. I arranged to get time off from the surgery and Phil and I spent ten wonderful days together really getting to know each other, going for long walks and dining out and visiting the theatre. We held hands constantly, neither of us wanting to let go of each other.

When the time came for Phil to leave I was overcome with sadness, but he assured me that he would get someone else to take over his position as soon as possible and that it would only be a matter of weeks before he returned permanently, so that we could have an autumn wedding, possibly at Caxton Hall. He left me in possession of a credit card and asked me to buy a lovely wedding outfit and anything I wanted for myself and Christopher. He said he would set me up with my own art studio if I wanted it in the future, as he knew that I was passionate about painting, and the recent fiasco at the art studio was just a temporary blip brought on by stress. We parted with Phil saying he would phone me regularly, and he gave me a number where I could reach him.

I tried to take in all that had happened in the past ten days, but somehow it did not seem real. I telephoned Mandy and told her what had happened and she was ecstatic. I asked her to meet me early in the afternoon of the next day in St James's Park, but first I wanted to go to the apartment in Westminster to have a look around.

I started off early in the morning with Christopher, because I was not familiar with the Westminster area and thought the apartment might be hard to find. I found the building after asking several people for directions. On approaching the main door I fumbled with the keys, feeling like an interloper.

I was about to insert the key in the lock when the door opened automatically. In the grand lobby there was a reception desk where a man sat peering over the top of his glasses; he had obviously let me in.

"Can I help you, madam?" he enquired.

"Oh, I think I'm in the wrong building,. I'm looking for apartment number twenty-eight." I was about to continue when he said, "You're in the right building, madam". Phil had obviously told him about me, as he seemed to be expecting me.

"You are Mrs Stevenson," he declared.

"Yes, that's right," I replied.

"Mr Rochford's apartment is on the first floor. The key you have in your hand is to the apartment. Go straight through the double doors to the lift which is on your right and you will find number twenty-eight on the first floor to your left."

I turned the key in the lock and was surprised to see a magnificent drawing room. My pictures were hanging on the wall, so there was no mistaking where I was. I let Christopher out of the pushchair and left it by the door, as I didn't want to spoil Phil's carpets, which looked very expensive.

I wandered around and gazed at all the wonderful foreign objects that Phil had on display. It was such a magnificent apartment, even better than the one in Belgravia. I turned around to see that Christopher had gone off somewhere, but I could hear the rustling of paper.

"Christopher, come here, where are you?" I called. I followed the rustling sound and found him sitting on the floor in the dining room, tearing at a parcel.

"Leave that alone, Christopher!" I shouted. But I was too late. He had unwrapped a shiny red model car, which Phil had thoughtfully left for him. I picked up the torn wrappings from the floor and found there was a card attached to the paper saying 'To Christopher, my very first present to you. I hope you like it. Philip'.

I put all the torn paper in a waste bin and got Christopher securely strapped in his push-chair. He was still clutching the red car, as he clearly wasn't about to give that up to anyone. I left the apartment, thanking the man sitting at the reception desk, and he got up and held the main door open for me to manoeuvre the pushchair out.

"Good day madam, I hope to see you again soon," he said. Phil had obviously had a chat with this man and I just wondered what he had said to him, as he was so very polite to me.

As we crossed from Horse Guards Parade, I saw Mandy sitting on the first seat in the park.

"My, hasn't he grown!" she said when she saw Christopher. "It must be nearly a year since I have seen you. How are you both?"

"We are very well and happy, thanks to you Mandy. I can't thank you enough," I said, giving her a big hug.

"Philip was sitting here when I spotted him reading a newspaper, what a bit of luck. Is everything OK now?" she asked.

"Phil came down to Surrey straight after your meeting with him, it was such a wonderful surprise.

We had so much to catch up on. It appears that he had to leave his home in Belgravia because his wife was making life impossible for him, and he moved temporarily to a rented apartment and that was the number I was ringing. Then the Westminster apartment came on the market and Phil snapped it up as our future home. He left Rex the new number on his second visit to the house, but unfortunately Rex didn't pass it on to me. Phil did say that Rex was getting into his car when he gave it to him, and knowing Rex, it's probably still lying in the glove compartment of his car. With Phil not hearing from me, and Rex telling him I had a new man in my life, he decided to take a posting abroad."

"What a mix up, darling!" Mandy said in amazement.

"Well, the main thing is we are at last together, or we will be pretty soon. Phil has asked me to marry him and to prepare for an autumn wedding. He's gone to the Middle East to tie things up and hand over the reins to someone else. Mandy, will you be my maid of honour?"

"Yes of course, you just try asking someone else!" she grinned.

"One day soon, when you're free, perhaps you'll come with me to pick out a wedding outfit and an outfit for yourself. I think Phil wants us to get married at Caxton Hall."

"Wow, that's where all the posh people get married. Well I suppose you'll be in that category now, posh and all. I don't suppose you'll want to be with your old mates once you're married!" Mandy said, with eyes downcast.

"Nonsense Mandy, I have been through too much hardship and sadness ever to think that my best mates don't count. They have been there for me all along. My feet are firmly on the ground and always will be, whatever happens once I'm married to Phil."

On returning home to Surrey I couldn't wait to tell Joyce all the good news. "Will you come to my wedding, Joyce?" I asked her.

"Of course I will, I'm so excited. The apartment sounds wonderful. Will you sell the cottage once you're married?" she asked.

"No, I'm going to keep it as a weekend retreat."

"Good idea. Maybe I could stay there during my summer holidays," she said. "If you're

not using it, that is!"

"Of course you can Joyce, come whenever you like."

"When is Philip coming back?"

"As soon as he can - maybe a couple of weeks, I can't wait to see him. I feel like a schoolgirl waiting for her first date."

"I'm very happy for you both, and congratulations on your forthcoming wedding."

"Is there any news from Jane?" I asked, hoping against hope that my euphoria would not take a battering.

"Yes, but not too good I'm afraid, she seems very down these days. Her marriage is still floundering and she's thinking of moving out of the marital home. It sounds as if Don only wanted a mother for Simon and he sure enough picked on the wrong girl for that."

"Oh, I'm sorry to hear that. Did she say where she will go?"

"No, but she said to send you her love when I next speak to you."

"Has she said anything about coming home?" I asked hesitantly.

"No, I think she's cut all her ties with Britain.

Maybe she feels that if she comes back she'll have to face up to seeing her little boy, and she can't bring herself to do that."

"I won't send her an invitation to the wedding in that case. There seems no point in letting her know of my new found happiness. It wouldn't be fair under the circumstances."

"No I wouldn't mention it. I think she's chosen the path she wants to follow and we should leave it at that," Joyce replied in a resigned manner.

"I got a letter from Patrick saying he was leaving for Australia at the end of the week and to kiss Chrissy for him. He said that one day he would come back to take him on holiday. He wrote, 'I love you both very much. God bless you both'. Whatever anyone says, I have parted on friendly terms with both my exes, I'm not sure whether that's a good thing or not," I said.

"Oh I'm sure it's a good thing, Mary. Do look after yourself and I will be in touch very soon."

"Bye Joyce, I'll let you know about the wedding as soon as we have a date."

The next few weeks went by very quickly. Mandy and I had a wonderful time shopping for outfits for the wedding. I had chosen a cream suit and hat, while Mandy had picked out a delightful lilac-coloured suit; I thought she looked very beautiful in it. For Christopher I chose a white silk shirt to go with his blue suit and black patent buckled shoes, and he looked such a dear with his gorgeous blond curls.

Mandy helped me with the wedding arrangements, once we had a positive date when Phil would return. I phoned him constantly, checking over every detail with him about the venue, invitations, flowers and cars. It was to be a small and intimate wedding with just a few friends and family, with the reception being held at the Dorchester Hotel, where Phil and I would spend the night before flying off to Paris. Mandy said she would be happy to look after Christopher while we were on honeymoon for a week. She said it would be a pleasure to have him and to take walks with him in the park. I was so excited at the prospect of Phil and me spending time alone together. We planned to return to collect Christopher and head off to the Caribbean for two further weeks away, where it would be our first time as a real family together.

The wedding day was the most exciting day of

my life. I had never felt so happy. It was impossible to believe that after all the lies and cheating I would actually be settling down with this wonderful, handsome man, who clearly adored both me and Christopher, and we would be living in a fabulous apartment in the centre of London. It was hard to believe that such a thing could happen to someone like me, in her middle years; such things only seem to happen to young, beautiful women with a position. More than once I had to pinch myself to realize that it wasn't all a dream.

On arriving in Paris we went straight to the Hotel Prince de Galles, which was just off the Avenue des Champs Elysees, where we stayed for four nights. We visited the Arc de Triomphe and the Eiffel Tower and when we were walking hand in hand along by the River Seine Phil said he had booked us on a further flight to Rome for two days. What a wonderful surprise - Paris and now Rome. I would be able to see all the sights that I had read about over the years, but never dreamt that I would ever see.

In Rome we visited the Coliseum and the Trevi Fountain. I couldn't resist throwing several coins over my shoulder into the fountain, which is supposed to bring luck and ensure your return. Phil also took me to see the Palazzo dei Conservatori exhibits and I thought Caravaggio's 'Gypsy Fortune-Teller' painting was magnificent.

My thoughts soon turned to Christopher, as we had never been apart before. Phil also sensed I was missing him and said we should leave Rome to collect him and continue our honeymoon in the Caribbean.

Christopher squealed with delight when he saw Phil and me, and there were big hugs and kisses all round. Mandy said she had enjoyed looking after Christopher and taking him to feed the ducks in the park.

We bundled Christopher into our car and took him to the apartment, where we repacked for our Caribbean holiday. Christopher helped with the packing by ramming several toys into a small case with his name on it. He thought he could also put toy cars and helicopters in it, but we had to explain to him that only a few soft toys were allowed.

Our first stop was Barbados, and then on to the many islands. Christopher loved to watch the ships sailing on the turquoise sea. I could have just kept going, as I felt so happy with the two people I loved most in all the world by my side in paradise. I didn't want the honeymoon to end, ever.

It was Phil's first visit to the Caribbean and he became entranced with the islands and said he wanted to buy a villa in Barbados as a holiday home. When we returned there we began to look around villas which were up for sale, and one in particular caught his eye. We brought back with us many brochures and Phil spent his time on the flight back home going through them.

On the way home I fell asleep and dreamed that I was home alone at night except for Christopher, and I was so glad when I awoke to find that Phil was still by my side. I squeezed his hand to make doubly sure and he kissed me on the cheek. Phil said he had never felt such happiness in all of his life as he did right now.

"I fell in love with you the first time I saw you at the exhibition," he said. He kissed me gently and I snuggled up to him, resting my head on his shoulder. I thought of how we had both met at the art exhibition and realized that I was eager to start painting again.

I now had plenty of ideas about what to paint, and I could almost see the exotic scenes coming to life on the canvas. I had so many subjects I wanted to paint and I was sure I would be kept busy for a very long time. I wanted to capture on canvas the lovely sights of Jamaica, which I would call an emerald island, as that was the true colour of this beautiful paradise.

On returning home we soon settled into our magnificent apartment and managed to get Christopher into a new nursery. Phil said he wanted to put Christopher's name down for Westminster School. I thought he was far too young, but he said that there was such a demand for places at the school that some couples were applying for their children as soon as they were born, as it was such a prestigious school. I was happy just to let Phil take charge, and was enormously grateful that he had Christopher's best interests at heart.

CHAPTER 7

Phil was true to his word and managed to find me a studio not too far away from Christopher's nursery. A friend of his knew about a space which had been used for a while as a small warehouse, just off one of the side roads which had originally been a stable. It was perfect, and I asked Mandy to come and look at it to see what she thought about it.

Mandy was a very good artist herself and we decided to work together in the small studio as soon as Phil had had it cleaned and repainted.

I began to paint in earnest all that lovely scenery that I had stored in my memory while on honeymoon. My brush strokes were flowing and my canvas soon began to fill with brilliant colours, the exceptional verdant and fresh scenery of Jamaica and the sights and scenery of the many islands we visited. Before long I had ten paintings to exhibit and was anxious to see if anyone would like to buy them. Phil thought they were exceptional and wanted to keep all of them, but I said I wanted to exhibit them along with the portraits that Mandy had so splendidly captured on her canvases.

The day before the exhibition I had a call from Joyce saying that she had heard from Jane, who was in the process of getting a divorce. Apparently things were getting very acrimonious between her and Don, and the short break apart which they hoped would bring them closer together had not worked; instead it had finished the marriage.

As Don was very wealthy he was trying to hold on to all of his assets. He had several houses dotted about the USA and abroad and was not about to part with any more than the absolute minimum to his wife, who he now saw as a cantankerous little bitch. He was only willing to allow her a very small amount in the divorce settlement, which he knew he would have to do because of his adultery.

Jane, on the other hand, said she wanted half his wealth, and Don had become very bitter, pointing out that he already had most of his assets before they had even met. Their lawyers had been battling for a couple of months and every time an offer was made, Jane turned it down. Knowing Jane, once she dug her heels in and made up her mind about something, nothing in the whole wide world could change her mind.

"Mary, I told Jane that she hadn't been married long enough to get half his money, but she feels so hurt and used over the little boy that she's going to release all the gossip on him that she has, and things could turn even more nasty," Joyce said.

"I feel so bad for Jane" I replied. "I hate hearing about this messy situation, especially right now, when things are going so well for me. I guess she'll be able to pull herself out of this, and the sooner the better as far as I'm concerned. She shouldn't be so greedy. She should settle with Don as soon as possible and move on. I don't want to phone her, she never listens to what I have to say, but please keep me informed, Joyce."

"Don't worry, I will. There's one other thing, Mary," Joyce said hesitantly. "I don't know how to say this, as I was so flabbergasted at the time to hear this from Jane, but she asked me how Christopher was doing!"

"What? I don't believe this! Why is she asking about Christopher, after almost four years of not wanting to know him or ever see him?" She didn't even ask about him when we were in New York."

"I know, but I thought I should mention it, just in case."

"In case what?" I yelled.

"Oh, I don't know, but I have a funny feeling about this. Jane is so unpredictable and is hurting right now, and she seems to be lashing out at everybody."

"Well let her lash out, but you can tell her from me, if she asks about Christopher again, that he is doing well and he's a happy and stable boy living with his mummy and daddy."

"OK Mary, I won't speak to her about Christopher unless she asks me again and I'll tell her just what you've told me. Don't worry about anything, I'll try to be there for Jane unless she abuses my friendship. I'll send her your love, if that's OK?" Joyce said.

"Yes Joyce, that will be all right. I still feel a little

bit of resentment towards her because of the decision she made about Christopher at the time of his birth," I blurted out.

After speaking to Joyce, I sat staring at the telephone. Why on God's earth had Jane now decided to focus on Christopher? Was it because she had been looking after Don's son Simon, and now she was losing him? Was it because she had learned what it feels like to be a mother?

I was still in a bit of a daze when Phil arrived back from the park with Christopher, covered in mud after playing football.

"Hello Mummy, can I have something to eat?" said Christopher. I hugged him to me in spite of his muddy clothes. "Yes my darling, but only biscuits and milk until after you've had a bath."

Phil marched Christopher off to the kitchen, saying "Come on my son, let's not make the furniture and carpet dirty."

Christopher really was Phil's son in almost every sense of the word. Phil would play with him, read to him and sit patiently trying to teach him to read. I loved watching them interact with each other. They were a joy to watch and I dearly loved both my 'guys'.

That evening I must have been absorbed in my thoughts, because Phil said, "What's wrong Mary? You've hardly spoken a word all evening. I know you very well. Something has upset you. Have I done something wrong?"

I told Phil that Joyce had telephoned and told him everything she had said about Jane asking after Christopher.

"Oh, I'm sure there's nothing to worry about" he said. "After all, you legally adopted Christopher, so there's no way she could ever think she could walk back into his life now."

"So why do I have this awful feeling that something dreadful is about to happen?" I said.

He took my hand in his and kissed it lightly. "Please put these thoughts out of your mind, nothing is going to happen" he said. "We are his parents now, and I would defy anyone who would try to take Christopher away from us."

As the weeks went by I tried to settle down and started painting some new canvases in the studio. Mandy and I were very fortunate in that nearly all our paintings had been sold at the last exhibition, so we had to work really hard to get a new collection together.

"What's that you have painted? Mandy asked, "I can't really make out what it is."

It seemed that whenever I was worried and upset, my artistic flair failed me. I told Mandy about Jane and said I was concerned.

"There are two things you can do," said Mandy, who was very clever at sorting things out. "One, you can forget about this whole thing with Jane. Or two, talk to Jane yourself and try to find out what she is up to. Personally I would ignore her. She sounds bitter and upset and wants everyone else to feel her pain in whatever way she can by thrusting this upon her close relatives. Now sort yourself out darling, and I would suggest you throw this canvas away and start afresh."

Mandy and Phil were right of course, and I decided to ignore Jane.

Life was gradually getting back to normal when Joyce rang again.

"Hello Mary, I thought I would let you know that Jane's been on the phone to say that Don has not given in to her with regard to her demands, and she should expect only a small settlement from the divorce. He says it's because they have only been married for just over two years and there are no children from the marriage. Needless to say Jane is hopping mad, especially knowing that Don is loaded."

I listened to Joyce without saying a word. I was wondering what was coming next.

"Are you still there, Mary?" she asked.

"Yes, I'm here Joyce. What does she intend to do now?" I asked, half dreading the reply.

"She said that after the decree nisi comes through she's going to come to Britain. She asked if she could stay with me for a while. She knows all about your new handsome, wealthy husband. I, like a fool, told her all about him, that was before I knew about her break-up. I think I should warn you Mary that she said she intends to see Christopher."

"Well, I'll have to see about that. I'm not sure that I want her to muddy the waters now, after all that has gone before."

"Don't get upset Mary, but Jane said to me that you forced her to give Christopher up before she'd had time to really make up her mind properly. She said that if someone had been able to talk to her and advise her on the matter, as she was very young, she would never have given Christopher up for adoption."

"That's a lie. I can't believe what I'm hearing, Joyce! You know very well what happened at the time the baby was born and how I begged her repeatedly to keep him," I said vehemently.

"I know, Mary. I was there, remember! I think she has an ulterior motive. She may be planning to extort money from Phil. I have to say she lied to me many times when she was living with me, so I know exactly what she is capable of. I also know that she needs money badly if she wishes to continue the lifestyle she's been used to of late in the United States. She certainly isn't getting it from the divorce settlement."

"After hearing that, Joyce, I do not wish to see Jane ever again. I know she's my daughter, but I can't be a mother to someone who still insists on going through life telling lies. Thank you for telling me all this." I was resigning myself to the fact that Jane was no longer the daughter I once knew and only someone who could bring pain and sorrow to my family.

I put the phone down and burst into tears. Jane had obviously not spared my feelings. She must have known how this would traumatise me. I felt that my heart had been ripped out. I had not just lost my daughter, but now felt that I would have to battle to keep my son.

In the small hours of that night, Phil, realising I wasn't in bed with him, opened the door of the office to find me sitting on the floor in the middle of the room surrounded by files and papers.

"What on earth are you doing darling?" he asked. "It's two in the morning. What are you looking for?"

"Christopher's adoption papers. I put them in a box, and now I can't find them," I said.

"Can't this wait until morning sweetheart?" he asked.

"No. I must find them. I didn't want to worry you, but Jane has been on the phone to Joyce again and she wants to see Christopher. She's been telling lies, saying that she didn't want Christopher adopted."

"Well my darling, she can say whatever she likes, it doesn't matter," Phil said, trying to pacify me.

"Yes it does, Phil. She may fight me for him. What if I have lost the adoption papers?" I was shaking like a leaf.

"Well you can get another copy, just like you can get a copy of your birth certificate or a death certificate," Phil said, holding me by my shoulders as if I was a child.

"No, I want to find the original papers." Nothing he said would appease me at this time.

"OK, my darling, where did you have the papers last?"

"I remember I had them at the time of Christopher's christening."

"Would Patrick have taken them?"

"Do you think he would? Surely not." I was trying to remember what had happened that day.

"It's possible. Anyway, why not give him a ring tomorrow and ask him?"

I went on rummaging through the drawers.

"What are you looking for now?" Phil asked. He was beginning to tire of my obsession over the papers.

"My address and telephone book," I said. "I'm going to ring him now, it's morning in Australia."

Phil threw both his hands in the air in

resignation. "OK my darling. I will go and make you a nice cup of tea and then when you have spoken to Patrick perhaps you will come back to bed."

I found the telephone book and looked up Patrick's number. A woman's voice answered.

"Hello, may I speak to Patrick? This is Mary." I said.

"How nice of you to phone Mary, this is Martha. Are you keeping well? How's little Chrissy?" she asked.

"He's very well and growing up fast, I'll send you some recent snaps of him. Is Patrick there?"

"No he's not here Mary," Martha said hesitantly, "Can I help?"

"I need to speak to Patrick rather urgently, do you know when he will be back?"

"I'm not sure at the moment, you see, Patrick has gone to the hospital." There was a long pause before she continued. "Patrick is having treatment," she said.

"Treatment! For what?"

"Mary, I'm sorry to tell you that Patrick is having chemotherapy. He has cancer."

There was a few seconds of silence.

"Cancer! When was he diagnosed with that?"

"Eight months ago now," came the reply.

"Oh my god! What is the prognosis"? I asked, not wanting to hear the reply.

"Not good, I'm afraid. They have only given him a year. We are trying to make his life

as comfortable as possible." I gasped in shock.

"Don't cry Mary, he wouldn't want you to be upset," she said.

At that moment Phil walked in with a cup of tea and saw how distressed I was. He put the tea down on the desk and put his arms around me. After a few moments I managed to collect myself and asked Martha to give Patrick my love and blessings, and a big kiss from Christopher. Then I explained why I had called.

"Martha, would you please ask Patrick if he knows what happened to Christopher's adoption papers, as I can't find them. Will you do this for me?" I asked.

"Of course I will. Don't worry, Patrick is quite strong still, and the chemo is working, perhaps he might beat this thing, who knows."

"Oh I do hope so, I'm so sorry to hear this news and I hope things will improve. All my love to you, Betty and Susan and kisses from Christopher. God bless you all."

I buried my head in Phil's chest and howled out loud.

"What's happened? he asked.

"I can't believe it. Patrick's been diagnosed with cancer. They say he might only have a short time to live."

"Oh my God! As if you haven't got enough to worry about." Phil hugged me to him. Then he put me back to bed after giving me two sleeping tablets.

"Trust me" he said, "things will sort themselves out darling, you'll see."

"Oh Phil, Christopher's mother is giving me grief and now his father is dying!"

"My darling, we are Christopher's parents now, and that's all you need to think about. Rest, and tomorrow things will look a whole lot better."

A few days later the phone rang very early one morning. It was Patrick.

"I hope I haven't got you out of bed," he said

apologetically. "I rang to let you know that I have got Chrissy's adoption papers, I think the vicar gave them to me. I think when I moved they were with some other papers of mine which were bundled up and put into a suitcase. I'll have them posted to you as soon as possible. Martha said you sounded very stressed about something, do you want to tell me about it?"

Trying to hold back the tears on hearing Patrick's voice and knowing what he was going through, I cleared my throat and said, "Oh, it's Jane. After all this time, she has now decided to start thinking about Christopher and wants to see him. She's accusing me of making her give him up."

"What bloody nonsense, after all you did to try to persuade her to keep the baby!"

"Yes, I know, but she is so angry and frustrated at the moment, because she's been going through a messy divorce and she's lashing out at everyone. That's what made me look for the adoption papers, just to reassure myself that everything was in order, and I panicked when I couldn't find them."

"You have nothing to worry about Mary, nothing at all," Patrick said without hesitation.

At this moment Phil came out of the bathroom wrapped in a towel after having a shower. He sat on the bed wondering who I was talking to at this hour of the morning. I mouthed 'Patrick' and put the phone on speaker so that he could listen to the conversation.

"Mary, when I think back now I realize what a fool I was," Patrick said. "I had everything, you and Chrissy, how happy we all could have been, and I threw it all away. You deserve to have a wonderful life and I wish you Philip and Chrissy every happiness in the future. Take care, Mary. I'll always love you and Chrissy. Bye for now, kisses to Chrissy. You'll get the papers straight away, I promise."

Before I could ask about his illness, Patrick had put the receiver down. I guess he didn't want to speak about it.

Phil and I sat on the bed for a few moments not speaking, just looking at one another.

"He does have the adoption papers thank God and he's having them posted to me straight away," I said.

"Now will you stop worrying please?" Phil said, hugging me to him.

Soon after that I heard from Joyce that Jane had arrived in Britain and had been staying with her temporarily until she found a place of her own. Joyce found out that Jane had gone to the adoption agency and thought she would rope Patrick into helping her gain access to Christopher, but when she was told that Mr and Mrs Patrick Stevenson had officially adopted the baby she was dumbfounded. She couldn't get her head round the fact that her mother had married the father of her baby. Joyce said she had gone berserk.

Jane then proceeded to say to the adoption agency that Mr Patrick Stevenson was the real father of her child and had raped her when she was 15 years old. The adoption agency then pointed out to her that she had signed official papers saying that the father was unknown. She then said to them that she wanted a DNA test to prove that he was the father and that he and her mother had secretly agreed to adopt the baby behind her back and that she wanted him back.

"What did you say to her, Joyce?" I said.

"I kicked her out of my home immediately and said she was telling a pack of lies, and that you and

Patrick only got together initially because Christopher was going to be adopted by strangers and neither of you could bear the thought of losing him. I don't think you will hear from her again Mary, at least I hope not." There was what sounded like a sigh of relief in her voice.

After a week had gone by, true to Patrick's word, I received the adoption papers from Australia. When I rang him to say that I had got them and to thank him, Martha answered the phone.

"Hello Mary, I'm sorry to tell you this, but Patrick passed away peacefully last night in his sleep. The family here and in the UK are all overcome with grief as you can imagine. The funeral will be some time next week. We have purchased a large burial plot for the family and as soon as the death certificate is available I'll send you one." Her voice was so very sorrowful.

"Oh my God, I can't believe it. I'm so sorry Martha!" I replied, with tears welling up in my eyes. I tried to get my head around why she thought I would want Patrick's death certificate, but before I could fathom this out she said, "You will need the certificate if Philip wants to officially adopt Chrissy." Of course, I hadn't thought of that.

"Thank you very much Martha. I don't know what to say, please accept my condolences, and I want to thank you for all your help. I haven't forgotten about the photos of Christopher, I'll send them to you soon. I send my love to Susan, Betty and you Martha, God bless. Please let me know the date of the funeral."

I took a breakfast tray into Phil, who was sitting up in bed. He took one look at me and knew straight away what had happened. After placing the tray down on the side table he took me in his arms and tears came rolling down my face as I confirmed what he already suspected.

After a while he said, "Well, if Jane wants Patrick's DNA now, she will have to dig for it."

I received news of the date of the funeral from Martha and arranged to send a beautiful wreath of flowers through Interflora from me and Phil, and another arrangement formed in the word 'Daddy' in colourful flowers from Christopher. I rang Joyce to give her the sad news and told her what Phil had said. She repeated that I should forget about what

Jane had said and to get on with my life, and that was exactly what I intended to do.

I resolved to put all the lies and worries behind me as soon as I received Patrick's death certificate. Phil said he would arrange to adopt Christopher as his son officially as soon as it was possible.

Some months later, when papers were filed, Phil was able to become Christopher's new adoptive father, and he was renamed Christopher Stevenson-Rochford.

CHAPTER 8

It was the weekend, a Sunday, and I didn't remember most of the events which had taken place the day before, but Phil had sat with me in the apartment patiently filling in the missing time which I had spent under a state of amnesia. He told me that I had been taken to hospital when I had been found crying in the park the day before and he revealed what happened.

When I arrived at the hospital I could not give any correct information about who I was or where I lived.

"I want you to keep still while I insert a needle into the back of your hand," the nurse said. "It will be just a small pinprick. I need to take a blood sample."

"Where am I?" I asked.

"You're in University College Hospital. Can you tell me your name?"

"Of course. I am Mrs Mary Stevenson."

"Do you remember your date of birth?" the nurse asked.

"The first of November."

"And how old are you, Mary?"

"I'm forty-four. How did I get here?"

"An ambulance brought you here. Do you remember being in an ambulance, Mary?"

"No. Why am I here?"

"You were found in a distressed state in St James's Park. You were confused and not very coherent. You were crying and asking someone to go away. Do you remember being in the park?" The nurse went on with her questions.

"No, I don't remember."

"We have given you a CT scan and an ECG," the nurse had informed me.

"What for?" I had asked tearfully.

"Just in case you have had a mini stroke. Do you remember having the scan or the ECG?"

"No, I don't remember."

"Where do you live, Mary?" the nurse persisted.

"In a cottage in Surrey," I replied.

"Do you have a telephone number so that we can ring someone?"

"No, I live alone." I was becoming hysterical by this time with all the questioning.

"Now don't cry, Mary. There is nothing to worry about. You are safe here. Your tests show that you have not had a mini stroke, and you don't have any heart problems either. You have what is known as TGA, that is transient global amnesia. Something upset you Mary, and it's sent you into a state of shock. We have found an address book in your handbag and we have telephoned a Mr Philip Rochford, who lives in Westminster. Does that name mean anything to you?" the nurse asked.

The name sounded vaguely familiar, but I couldn't think why, and I didn't answer the nurse.

"He will be here in just a short while. Meantime, just rest, Mary" she said.

When Phil arrived at the hospital, the sister in charge explained that I had been found in St James's Park, suffering from amnesia. Apparently I was alone and crying on a seat.

"But there should have been a little boy with her, our son Christopher," Phil had insisted. "Where on earth is he?"

The nurse said to Phil that I was alone when a passer-by found me crying and called an ambulance. I had been incoherent and didn't know where I was. This was the first they had heard about a child.

Phil ran to the room where I was and seized me up in his arms. The nurse followed close behind.

"Darling, what happened, where is Christopher?" Phil said, not knowing that it was Christopher's disappearance that had caused the trauma. The nurse told Phil that I was still very confused and dazed. She made this clear to him by asking me "How old are you, Mary?" in front of him.

Again I replied "Forty-four".

"And where do you live, Mary?" she repeated her questions.

I replied "Surrey."

"Do you live with anyone?" the nurse pressed on with her questioning.

"No" I replied, "I live alone."

Phil was horrified. "Look" he said to the nurse, "my wife is 48 years old and she lives with me and our son in Westminster. She does have a cottage in Surrey which we use as a holiday home."

The nurse told Phil that I needed to rest, but he could stay with me. I would have to be monitored over the next few hours. Phil said he needed to phone the police to tell them of a missing child.

The police arrived at the hospital and interviewed Phil. He gave the police a photograph of Christopher which he always carried in his wallet, and told them that I had left the apartment at about 10.30 am with our son to go to St James's Park to feed the ducks. They then said that they would do everything to find him and put out a 'missing persons' alert. They would alert all the airports and railway stations in the area and would check CCTV cameras from 10.30 am onwards at Westminster station.

"Is there anyone you know who might snatch your son?" the officer asked.

"No, certainly not," Phil replied.

Phil then phoned Mandy to tell her what had happened, and she said to him she would go immediately to St James's Park to search for Christopher, just in case he was wandering around lost and crying somewhere. Phil also phoned Joyce to let her know what had happened.

"Jane, it's got to be Jane who took him!" Joyce said. "She phoned me last week to say she was thinking of going to London. I didn't tell you because I didn't want you to worry."

"Well we don't know that for sure, but I'll tell the police to keep a lookout for her," Phil said.

Apparently it was not until about eight o'clock in the evening that I was able to start thinking straight, and I kept on saying "Why am I here?" I still could not remember the events of the day. I couldn't even remember leaving the apartment in the morning.

"Where's Christopher, where's my son?" I started to scream.

"He's OK, he is with a neighbour," Phil lied, not wanting me to go into another state of shock.

The nurse told Phil that they had carried out a CT scan, just in case I had any bleeding in the brain, which would suggest a mini-stroke. They also informed Phil of the other tests which they had carried out and said they were going to keep me in hospital overnight for observation. I still couldn't account for the missing hours of that day, but I was told that I shouldn't worry about this as I would probably get my memory back in full in time, and even if I didn't, I would suffer no permanent harm, and that TGA is not as rare as one might think.

Joyce arrived early on Sunday morning and while Phil made his way to the hospital to collect me, she went to Westminster Police Station to go through pictures taken by the CCTV cameras at Westminster Station the day before. There were hundreds of pictures of people on the platform at the station and it was not easy to spot a small boy of Christopher's age. After two hours the police and Joyce had not been able to find any sign of him in the crowds.

While Joyce was taking a break, Mandy arrived. She had had no luck in the park the day before. Although she had stopped many visitors to the park and showed them a picture of Christopher, no one could recollect seeing him. She had spoken to many mothers who said that earlier in the day there were a lot of children playing near a big tree. They were chasing each other round the tree and the mothers couldn't say who the children were.

"How's it going? anything yet?" Mandy enquired.

"No, not yet. But I'm pretty sure Jane is behind all this," Joyce replied. "We have looked at hundreds of pictures taken at Westminster Station, but we couldn't spot Christopher in any of them."

"How about looking at CCTV footage at Green Park Station?" Mandy suggested.

"Is that nearby?" Joyce asked, as she was not familiar with the area.

"Yes, if you're in St James' Park and you cross the Mall, you're in Green Park."

"OK, let's go and ask for the pictures taken yesterday at Green Park Station and we can both go through them together." Joyce grabbed her coat and she and Mandy rushed to the Mall to cross to Green Park.

"Wow! Is that Buckingham Palace?" Joyce asked Mandy.

"Yes," replied Mandy.

"It's bigger than I thought it was, just sitting there at the end of the Mall. Wow!" said Joyce in amazement.

"Well I'd love to take you sightseeing later, after we have found Christopher!" Mandy retorted.

Joyce and Mandy searched the CCTV footage taken the day before of the passengers at Green Park Station as they entered the platform. After a while Mandy shouted, "There, look there! Is that Christopher?" The machine was stopped and rewound and Joyce and Mandy peered closely at the picture. Sure enough there was my little boy. A slim blonde woman of about twenty to twenty-five years of age was holding him by the hand.

"Is that Jane?" Mandy asked.

"I'm not sure, Jane has dark hair. But I'm pretty sure that is Christopher."

The police were alerted and at each station after Green Park in both directions, video images were checked to find out at which station the woman with Christopher had got off. Joyce phoned the hospital to let Phil know that they had spotted Christopher on the platform at Green Park Station and that the police were trying to track down the movements of a blonde woman in her twenties who had a little boy with her.

Phil was not at the hospital as he had taken me home, so she phoned the apartment and he was very relieved at hearing the news. Joyce and Mandy then headed back to our apartment in Westminster.

Shortly after that the police rang to say that a young woman had been spotted at Bank Station with a small boy answering the description of Christopher. "She seems to be heading east and we have alerted the staff at Stratford Station just in case she is hoping to pick up a coach to Stansted Airport," the officer told Phil. "We already have police patrolling all the London airports just in case she is trying to leave the country."

Sure enough the woman was spotted at Stratford Station, but the police lost sight of her from there. Phil left the apartment with Mandy and headed straight for Stansted Airport, while Joyce stayed with me to try to comfort me. I was pretty fragile after leaving hospital and I'm just glad I didn't remember too much about the whole episode. I was refusing to eat and kept pacing the floor in a state of anxiety.

Joyce said we should go out for a breath of fresh air, and she kept in touch with Phil by phone. I asked her where Christopher was, and Joyce said that Phil had gone to collect him from a neighbour. I believed her.

For three hours there was no more news of Christopher. Plain-clothes police had been watching the airport. They had checked passenger lists and everyone who had checked in for flights with small children.

The breakthrough came when the police were alerted by a crying child on a flight to Italy who said he wanted his mummy. The airport staff were suspicious of the young lady who said she was his mother, and showed them what looked like genuine passports for both of them. She was let through passport control and was now in the departure lounge.

The airport staff pointed out to the police a dark-haired woman with a crying child. At first they thought that this was not the woman they were looking for, but on closer inspection the boy certainly looked like the missing child.

"Hello, what's your name?" a plain-clothes police officer asked the small boy as he sat down beside him.

"Christopher."

"Would you like a sweet, Christopher?"

"Yes please" he answered. The police officer gave Christopher a sweet and signalled to other plain-clothes detectives, who approached from the rear and told the woman that they wanted to speak to her alone. They led her away and an officer told her, "You are under arrest for the kidnapping of Christopher Stevenson Rochford." They read her her rights before taking her away for questioning.

One of the police officers asked Christopher if he wanted to ride in his police car to go and see Mummy and Daddy, and he said 'Yes please', with a wide grin. As they were leaving the airport Phil had arrived with Mandy, and he scooped little Christopher up in his arms and kissed him on both cheeks.

"I'm going to have a ride in a police car, Daddy, do you want to come?" said Christopher.

Phil said, "Daddy has to drive his car home, but Mandy will come with you and I'll see you at home. I'll be right behind you."

When Jane was questioned, her bag was searched and they found the blonde wig which she had been wearing. She had used the passport of her ex-husband's son, having replaced the photograph with that of Christopher's. It seemed that she had been stalking us for some time so she could take Christopher's photograph and use it to replace the picture of Don's son on his passport, as it was highly unlikely that she had taken it the day she snatched Christopher.

Phil telephoned Joyce to say that Christopher was safe and that they would be home soon.

Joyce and I were waiting in the lobby of the Westminster apartment after our walk when Phil and Mandy arrived back. Mandy whispered to Joyce, "Why do you think Jane was heading for Italy?"

With a shrug of her shoulders Joyce replied, "Well, I'm sure she must still have friends out there from her modelling days."

"I'm so glad to see you, Mummy," said Christopher.

I hugged my son to me and felt an enormous calming feeling come over me.

Later on Sunday evening I settled Christopher down with his favourite toys and asked Phil where he had been. It was then that he told me what had really happened. He had found out that Jane had taken Christopher from the park the day before and spent the night with him at an hotel near the airport ready to catch a flight to Italy today.

Through tears of joy, at finding everything was all right with my family, I asked Phil what he thought would happen to Jane.

"Oh don't you worry about her right now," he said sternly.

Some time later we heard that Jane had been treated leniently and given a one-year suspended prison sentence, on the grounds that she had been suffering the trauma of her recent divorce and the loss of her stepson. She had been ordered not to contact Christopher again.

Once again I was in floods of tears, knowing what my daughter had put me through and that an even wider gap had now been created between us. Phil put his arms around me.

"Thank God you and Christopher have come out of this unscathed," he said. "Let's just put all this behind us and try to live a happy life together."

I knew that I would never again have to be alone.